THE CAPTAIN'S CHRONOLOGY

The nine lives of an extraordinary cat

Simon Robinson

The Captain's Chronology is a work of fiction. Any reference to real people (living or dead), actual locales, and historical setting are used solely to lend the fiction an appropriate cultural and historical setting. All other names, characters, places, and incidents portrayed in this book are the products of the author's imagination, and any resemblance to actual persons living or dead is entirely coincidental.

For Louie Littlebones

and

for the Captain.

We miss you.

CONTENTS

I sit beside the fire and think

of people long ago,

and people who will see a world

that I shall never know.

But all the while I sit and think

of times there were before,

I listen for returning feet

and voices at the door.

J.R.R. Tolkien

THE DRUID OF MÔN

I open my eyes and I see everything. As I lie upon the soft sand, the moon is bright above me and I hear the gentle waters of Menai Straight caressing the nearby shore. It is a beautiful evening, a perfect evening on which to depart. When I close my eyes again I will return to the Otherworld, to Annwn and its cauldron of rebirth. But there is no rush, no hurry. I have time to tell you of the past, the present and the future; time to tell you of my companion—the star charmed cat called the Captain.

I was waiting under the new moon, staring up into the infinity of space. Knowing what to expect I sat in my customary spot upon a stone slab by the river. The sound of the waters diminished as I breathed deeply and the light appeared at the edge of the horizon.

I had seen it many times in the past as it flew through the sky like a tiny sun. Each time the visitor would come closer before shooting away again to dance among the constellations. This occasion, I knew, would be different; that something special would happen.

The light grew brighter as it arced through the spangled sky and I whispered an ancient greeting. I stood now, holding my yew staff high, and the light came racing on towards me, its burning tail crackling in the atmosphere. The forest glowed as the earth drew it closer and then it was upon me with the sound of thunder. I struck at the ground in the blinding light. I felt the power travel through me as the shooting star buried itself at my feet and the river waters exploded into steaming rain. I looked into the suddenly dry river bed where the star glowed deep in the ground below and then the waters rushed in again and filled the chasm with the sound of a long deep sigh. I sat again and closed my eyes in meditation.

For three days and three nights I waited by the deep pool. Images visited me of vast winged chariots upon the ocean, of a labyrinth of stone, of multitudes toiling in darkness, of iron eagles glinting in the sky, of giant snakes that hissed and screamed and finally, of myself lying still upon a sandy bank. On the fourth day I opened my eyes and looked about in the warm sunlight. The river, though changed, still flowed and the birds still sang in the trees.

I waited. Then, in the distance I saw movement. A boy was standing on the river bank holding out a black and white kitten. I heard his shrill laugh and saw the tiny splash as his hands opened and the kitten fell. I stood again and where my hands had pushed against the stone there remained their soft impression.

Born at the moment of the meteoric impact, the kitten had snuggled close to his mother before being ripped from her embrace. Now the chill water compressed his lungs as he bounced backwards over river stones and spun around in eddies. Instinctively he tried to swim but the rushing water overwhelmed him and his breath escaped with every jarring impact until he could struggle no more. His eyes were wide in the receding light as he sank into the depths of the deep pool. In the darkness he was surrounded by a ruby effervescence as the sky-rock glowed again with the accumulated heat of scorched atmosphere. The warmth filled him with the energy of instinct and he thrust out tiny limbs as I reached down to him.

Feeling his needle claws attach themselves to my hand, I drew him up towards the sun and out of the dark, deep pool. The gentle pressure of my bloodied fingers massaged the water from his sodden lungs and then I embraced him and he relaxed, feeling his exhausted body fill with breath. My face was close, my mouth upon his; breathing life into him until he gasped, and the world around him exploded into colour. He lay shivering in my arms as I carried him past the vicious boy who cowered from the power of my admonishing stare. I made our way through the oaken forest to its centre where a hushed glade welcomed our arrival. At the centre of the glade, my small round house, and at the centre of the house, a fire sprang up, next to which I laid the kitten gently in a small wicker basket lined with soft linen.

He slept as I watched over him, stroking his soft fur and whispering again and again the mantra of the ancient greeting. It was in this way, imbued as he was with the heat of the meteorite, my nourishing breath and the incantation of the ancestors that the kitten awoke, changed by the power of his young experience.

I carefully gathered him up and carried him out into the sunlight and the beauty of the garden of Britain. The oak grove whispered in the breeze as I set the kitten down on the soft grass. High above us a detached leaf fluttered in the sky and the kitten watched its slow rotating descent until it landed softly next to him.

He peered intently at it and then his tongue clacked in his mouth. "Le, le, le." His tiny bottom lip touched his sharp teeth. "Fa, fa, fa,"

I waited in astonished anticipation as he blinked his yellow eyes and opened his mouth soundlessly. He inclined his tiny head towards me. "Lef, lef, lef," he squeaked as I watched, breathless. "Leaf, leaf, leaf." The words, I knew, were swirling in his mind.

"Leaf many tray."

His progress stunned me and I sat down heavily beside him as the kitten's tongue clacked again and the words fell into order. "As many as leaves on a tree!"

I breathed deeply and looked at him with serious eyes. "Yes, as many as that," I said as the kitten looked back at me, his ears swivelling.

"What are they?" he bleated.

"They are words," I told him. "Wrought and burnished in the minds of people they can be used for good or ill. Use the words wisely my young friend and you will be like the brightest star in the sky."

We were inseparable. The little cat rode high on my shoulder as we walked through the forest collecting mushrooms. If we encountered people from the nearby village they would bow and I would smile and nod. The villagers knew me well. Their parents had known me, their grandparents had known me and before that, *their* parents had known me. I am an old, old man. They would stand hushed as we passed, listening as I whispered the ancient mantra to the kitten on my shoulder.

The warm days grew longer as the sun reached its midsummer zenith.

I sat in quiet meditation as the kitten pounced at grass stalks swaying in the breeze, or chased flies in haphazard flurries of excitement. Each day, he became more and more aware of the sounds of the forest. Sometimes he was frightened, but I would smile and tell him that he should not fear the present, for I had used a very old inducement to see far and knew what was to come. The invocation was powerful: it revealed a distant reality so clearly it was as though I were standing there in a crowded stone hall. I concentrated as I held my staff high in the air and then I threw my head back and laughed as I connected with my little friend's life to come. Striking at the ground with my staff I released the power of the meteorite into the future.

"Why do you strike the ground?" he asked.

"You will know. Far, far away, I can see you in time's distance. You are free!"

As always there were visits from the ancient spirit of the forest, my gentle old friend the Treeman. Because the little cat knew that there was nothing to fear, the Treeman, with his moss covered face and mistletoe beard, seemed very ordinary. The kitten would practice climbing among gentle limbs as we sat together in the glade, quietly talking and chuckling; remembering tales of giants and heroes.

Beneath the flaring oak trees I lay on my back in the soft, sweet emerald grass. My grey head was turned and I was smiling. I watched the little cat, amused that he looked like a white cat wearing a black cloak. I watched him preparing to pounce; shuffling his back feet with zealous instinct; coiling himself into a spring squeezed tightly with compressed energy. Ears pointing forward, there was a hush in a timeless place, and then the spring's release as the little cat launched himself through the air. He landed on a bobbing leaf, then tumbled over, chomping at it with tiny teeth.

I had never been more content but my happiness was poignant with the knowledge that as summer began to fade and the leaves turned to russet and brown, as inevitably as change will come, darkness approached. A darkness for which I had no solution.

On an overcast day in autumn, a small delegation of people came from the village to visit me. They were shy, wringing their hands, shuffling their feet as I invited them into the house. I knew why they had come. They pleaded with me to summon a dragon to guard the shore. I told them that the time for such things was long past, but that I would stand with them. They thanked me and left with tear-stained faces.

That evening, as we sat in the glow of the fire, peering into the embers, I stroked my friend's soft coat and quietly said, "Tomorrow, I have to leave you. I have to leave our garden."

He cried out, but I put my finger to my lips and he was hushed.

"How I value your innocence and your instinct," I said softly. "I am sad to part, but we must all leave in time."

"Where are you going?"

I smiled. "I must travel a familiar and much worn road. A road that you too, my young friend, must travel one day."

"I'm afraid."

"Recognize your fear for what it is: instinct. It is our nature. The sun will still rise, and though it may be changed, the world will continue to turn beneath its solar wheel. This is all we can know as we strike out upon the road. If we accept that, then we are free and great things can happen. I will ensure that here you will be protected, and if you wish it, we will be together again."

"When?" asked the cat with excitement.

"When the journeys are done. When the mysteries are revealed. When it is time."

We sat together for many hours that night staring into the fire as I recalled stories about the forest and the stones. About my travels to distant places, travels which had taken me to the realms of the living and the realm of the ancestors. I spoke of Annwn, the Otherworld, where I would wait for my little friend's return and where we would be together again.

"You will also make many journeys my young friend as you travel through the perfect chaos that people call time," I told him. "It has been my delight to meet you upon my last journey while you begin your very first. The bond between us is forged from love more powerful than any magic."

5

I placed my hand on his little head and I felt his mind dance with words.

"Remember," I said, "we are free."

He awoke in the blue enchantment of early morning. The silky light melted the shadows as night ebbed away and the first shimmer of dawn slanted through the windows. I was sleeping peacefully, with even breath, and the last fire embers twinkled like distant stars in the hearth. The air was still, and the little cat could smell the sweet freshness of the dew. Quietly, he climbed down from the bed and made his way out into the glorious dawn. The forest had never smelt so good or seemed so full of beauty. The sweet symphonic birdsong affirmed the power of our grove. He watched the finches and sparrows flitting among the trees and then heard me behind him. He turned and saw that I was dressed and carried my staff. I bent down and picked him up.

"Time for me to go, but don't be afraid. I will not leave you all alone," I whispered.

I stroked his soft fur for the last time, kissed him and then set him back on the soft dewy grass. I smiled, winked, then turned, and disappeared into the forest. Everything had already been said.

The soldiers were many. They wore armour. They carried spears and shields. They drew their swords. They had come to bring civilization. They would cut down our sacred groves. They would show that Mars[*] was stronger than any British deity that dared to challenge his power. They gritted their teeth to hide their fear as they crossed the slack water of Menai Strait to our Ynys Môn.[†] They knew about the ancient legends of our place. They had heard stories about the Druids who lived here.

This was the last corner of ancient Britain, and these were the last hours of its keepers of traditional knowledge.

On the shore of the island a desperate crowd of men and women had

---

[*] Mars (Martis) was the name of the Roman God of war.
[†] From Welsh the English translation is *Isle of Mona* today called the *Isle of Anglesey*. The island has a long and ancient association with Druids.

gathered to defend their home. They were not cowed by the overwhelming odds that they faced, but were inspired and fearless, as people are when they have run out of time. They knew that the soldiers would be ruthless in the execution of their orders. Orders to make an example. To shock. To burn. To kill.

When the invaders landed at the shore of our island they were engaged with ferocity, but smarting from the shame of their fear, the soldiers were ruthless in their killing so that the glistening shore of Ynys Môn was stained with blood.[*]

With more and yet more of the attackers jumping from their boats, the conflict was decided as inevitably as the tide will flow. At the centre of the milling, dwindling crowd I stood quietly waiting. I knew that among the invaders Alexios was coming, and I was remembering him:

Thirty summers ago, as a child, under the Greek sky, under the enormous moon, Alexios had stood among the vines, looking up. Holding out his hands, stained red with grape pulp he had wondered what lay in the future for these young stained hands, dark in the moonlight. He heard his mother calling him to dinner after the grape harvest, her voice and the sounds of celebration and laughter warm in the still evening. Walking towards the stone house, his innocent heart full of joy, Alexios turned again to the glowing moon and paused to imagine faraway places and the people who were also blessed by its silver light.

I saw it all with clarity, for in that moment, in a grove of oak trees many miles away and across the sea, I looked up into the sky with eyes that glistened with prophetic tears and whispered, "I forgive you."

We are joined by fate, Alexios and I, and since that moment when I first sensed his presence, as he sensed mine, I have felt his deepening pain. What turned his joy into rage? He became a victim of his desire for adventure. His mother had pleaded with him to stay but the army offered him the chance to travel to the faraway places that he dreamed of. When he returned he found his homeland scorched by invasion. The farm had been burned, the vines destroyed, his family murdered.

---

[*] These events of the year 61AD, under the direction of the Roman General, Gaius Suetonius Paulinus, are recorded by the Roman historian, Tacitus. See the *Annals,* Book XIV, Chapter 30.

He rejoined the army and carried his mothers face in his mind as he replicated the violence of her end again and again with a cold and vengeful heart.

This merciless warrior was now a veteran of many campaigns. I recognised him as he cut a swath through the crowd with murderous efficiency, his short sword stabbing and ripping. Then we were face to face at last and he paused for a moment before striking hard at me. As he dealt the fatal blow I gripped his hand upon the hilt of his sword, looked into his eyes and asked him,

"What lay in the future for these red stained hands?"

Recognition flickered across his face and his mouth turned down. He trembled. He was like a child who kills a squirrel with a stone and then kneels, weeping with remorse.

The strength left my old legs and I quietly lay down. Alexios knelt beside me. I looked up and whispered so that he drew close to hear. I blessed him with ancient power and promised him, "You are innocent. I forgive you."

His scarred and rugged face was set in a dark frown, and then, from deep within him came a wrenching gasp. For the first time in a very long time he wept and held my hand. As I weakened, my hand opened, revealing a scrap of parchment paper and, oblivious to the terrible sounds and shrieks around him, he held the paper. Upon it he saw my simple drawing of a small round house surrounded by trees with a black and white cat at the doorway. Beneath, neatly written, was this word:

Sanctuary

My little cat, I knew, was shivering. He felt alone. Sitting with his paws tucked under him in the doorway, his eyes were wide as he smelled the burning in the air and heard the distant crack of axe upon tree. There were shouts and screams in the forest and his ears were flattened in fear. He worried about me and talked to himself for reassurance.

Throughout the day, the smoke became thicker and the violent sounds came closer. He heard splits and snicks echo around him as terrified deer crashed through the forest. Then, something large loomed into view, and he cried out as the Treeman appeared from the woods and stood in front of the house.

"Our friends are taken from us," said the Treeman sadly.

The kitten climbed up into the arms of the Treeman, nestled against him, and the two clung to each other.

The afternoon was late and dim when the soldiers arrived at the glade. Thirty of them stood in the clearing looking at our house. Their axes glittered in the flicker of their burning torches as they spread out and approached the Treeman, who to them, simply looked like a tree. My little friend shrunk back into the branches as two soldiers paused, drew breath, and struck again and again at the Treeman with such force that he groaned and shivered. The kitten squeezed his eyes shut and hung on tightly. Then, his heart pounding, he realized that the shaking had stopped. He opened his eyes and saw that the soldiers were gathered together, looking towards the edge of the clearing. There, imbued with my power and honed by war, an unstoppable figure stood in the darkness holding a sword in one hand and a piece of parchment paper in the other.

"Who's there?" yelled one of the soldiers.

There was a pause. The burning torches crackled.

"Leave this place," Alexios said quietly.

"Who are you?" shouted the leader of the soldiers.

"I protect this sanctuary."

The soldiers looked at each other and drew their swords.

"You are one against thirty," scoffed the leader, and smirking, looked around at his men. He gestured towards the Treeman. An axe was lifted and again it struck hard.

"*Stop it! Don't hurt my friend,*" shrieked my little cat.

The soldier stepped back in shock, looking up at large yellow eyes fixing him from above.

"There is witchcraft here," he gasped, and looking around at his startled comrades, he stumbled backwards. I saw that fear was kindled deep within them.

9

The figure at the edge of the forest reached behind him and smoothly mounted his shield upon his arm. He beat three times upon it with his sword and at a brisk walk, moved towards the soldiers. Their leader drew his own sword and struck at Alexios who moved so quickly, and with such agility, that he seemed to slow time. The leader's sword moved in a glinting arc through the empty air and with a flick of his arm, Alexios smashed the hilt of his sword into the man's face, sending him tumbling and bloodied to the ground.

"Leave this place," commanded my enchanted champion, pointing his sword at the leader who gathered himself up, glancing around for his men. Their discarded axes lay uselessly upon the grass. He swallowed, and then he too ran into the dark forest.

My kitten, I knew, sensed something of me about the stranger and yet he did not recognize him. Instinctively he knew that he was safe, that he was protected. Alexios knelt and slowly held out his large, hard hand and the little cat cautiously approached. My champion gently stroked the soft fur and quietly raised the cat up, cradling him in his scarred arms.

Alexios will live in peace in the round house in the glade for many years with the cat he will call his Captain. He will lie in the soft grass and smile and they will talk and talk and talk.

I am a very old man so don't feel sad for me as I lie here dying. The sand is soft beneath me, the moon is bright above me and I hear the gentle waters of Menai Straight caressing the nearby shore. It is a beautiful evening, a perfect evening on which to depart. I will close my eyes and be in Annwn which lies but a breath away. I will close my eyes and leave you to the future past of the Captain's chronology, to the perfect chaos that people call time.

ADDENDUM TO *The Druid of Môn*

In the early hours of the morning, the Followers came. They knelt and hot tears stained their cheeks as they found the body of the old man resting on the sandy bank. This they bore away to a place of the old man's choosing, for he had given instructions on what must be done. At the place on the hill, they dug a round grave, and with slender fingers they wrapped the body in a heavy cloak, adorned with many shiny silver disks. They carefully and reverently placed an acorn in his mouth, as was his wish, and lay him in the ground. They stood quietly for a moment and said a prayer particular to them. Then they disappeared into the mist.

THE LAST BEAR IN BRITAIN

"My Lords, Ladies and Gentlemen, it is our privilege and pleasure to present to you, the great Artus, the last bear in Britain!"

The children squealed with delight and the townspeople hurrahed. The big brown bear was grinning as he danced forward with remarkable agility, and the musicians struck up their reedy tune to the hollow beat of a drum. The chains around the creature's limbs jangled as he hopped, dipped and danced like a Greek fisherman at a wedding. For ten years he had danced and he knew, or sensed, that he was a valued member of the travelling group of minstrels to which he belonged. They lived their life on the road, moving from village to village and from town to town in a ramshackle collection of brightly painted wagons. Each year, they followed the same route, as predictably as the earth orbits the sun. Eagerly anticipated, they would arrive in any given place to cheers of delight, and they would dance, and play music, and enthral.

Five years before, the Captain had been discovered by Brendan, the leader of the little group. Brendan was a jovial and kindly eccentric who had found the kitten crying in an oak tree in a violent thunderstorm. As the lightning had flashed and crashed around them, he had coaxed the frightened kitten down and placed him under his cloak where it was warm, safe and dry. The Captain had never forgotten this kindness in a harsh world and became Brendan's constant companion. The Captain loved his life and the minstrels loved the Captain. They always made a fuss of him and stroked his thick black coat until he purred and blinked his yellow eyes.

Three years after his rescue, on a summer's evening much like any

12

other, under a heaven filled with stars, the members of the little troupe sat around their camp fire. As was their pleasure, they were joking and telling their stories when something occurred that stunned this company of minstrels: the Captain spoke to them. Gwen had screamed, someone fell off a stool, and Brendan was uncharacteristically lost for words as the Captain informed them how happy he was to share their company. He blinked at their reaction and then told them in his broken English that he didn't know why, but that after listening to them he had realized that he too could speak. The words that he listened to seemed to him like colours in his mind, which over time, made sense of the sounds that he heard. When they had recovered from their shock, the minstrels asked question upon question. The Captain answered as best as he could, but in truth there was nothing that he could reveal of the world that was not already known. He was unable to account for his gift of voice.

That night, Brendan could not sleep for the excitement he felt as he invented a new entertainment which would involve the Captain. He realized that in this the year 900, a time of fear and persecution, it would be suicide to reveal the existence of a talking cat. He would find a way to present this singular talent by creating a great ventriloquist act that would make their fortunes!

The tune ended and Artus clapped his big paws together. He made satisfied grunts in response to the general applause and ambled back to his spot behind the stage where Gwen waited for him with food and water. Artus had been their companion for twelve years and a close bond had been forged. Brendan and Gwen had adopted him as a tiny cub after his mother had been killed by Saxon soldiers in a hunt. They had raised the cub by hand and he had been kept safe in their company. He was part of their family and was doted on like a child. The feelings were reciprocated, for Artus, intelligent and affable, was utterly content.

The murmuring, pink faced crowd surged forward to the stage with excitement as the minstrels played a mysterious tune of introduction.

"Ladies and Gentlemen, prepare now to travel back to the ancient days of Merlin and the time of magic!"

A curtain was swept aside and Brendan stood with his arms held aloft, wearing a great white cloak and long wizardly false beard. The assembled crowd gasped and clapped. On a table at centre stage, surrounded by "magical" bowls and liquids of dubious origin, sat the Captain. His white markings were covered with black make-up so that he looked every inch the witch's cat of storied legend.

"Behold!" cried Merlin in a loud, wavering, wizard voice which succeeded in hushing the crowd. "Behold! My spirit guide, as ancient as the Druids. Together, we will amaze and confound you."

"We will amaze and confound you," cried the Captain in a theatrical old crone voice that Brendan had coached him to use. Brendan comically moved his jaw so that his beard twitched enough that the adults in the audience were able to smile, confident that they knew this trick of belly talking. The children watched, wide-eyed.

The ventriloquist show was an unprecedented success for the minstrels and word of them spread across the country. The crowds that greeted them grew and grew as did the size of their purse. Soon, they were able to buy new wagons and afford grander costumes. The ventriloquist act became the main feature of their performance, enthusiastically applauded wherever the little company went. People began to travel to see them and one day, among the crowd, was one such gentleman dressed in fine clothes and riding the best of horses. Following the performance he approached Brendan who was still dressed in his wizard costume which now sported embroidered stars and moons.

"I very much enjoyed your performance," said the finely dressed man. "Word of your talents has spread far and I am sent by the King to invite you to his castle where you will perform for the royal household in seven days."

Brendan took a deep breath. He knew that the invitation was in fact a command and a refusal was out of the question. "We are most honoured and will prepare immediately," he said with feigned enthusiasm.

That evening there was heated debate over this turn of events, for the minstrels were Britons who had a natural distrust of all things Saxon.*

"What if he sees through the act?" gasped Gwen when she heard the news. "It's one thing to perform in a town square but at the Saxon

---

* The Angles and Saxons invaded Britain from the German regions of Angeln and Saxony in the 5th and 6th centuries in the wake of the withdrawing Romans and their failing Empire. The new invaders became known collectively as the Anglo-Saxons.

court?"

"Don't be worried," said Brendan with a wink. "People only see what they expect to see."

The next morning, filled with a disquieting sense of uncertainty, they set off for the Royal castle of Edward the Elder.[*] For several days they journeyed over hills and along narrow lanes and down long, broad, Roman roads. Their brightly painted wagons attracted slaves from the fields as they passed. Artus ambled along contentedly and would do a little dance if there were children watching him. They would giggle and clap their hands together and to their delight, Artus would bow.

At last they crested the brow of a hill and for the first time they saw the giant Saxon castle squatting in the valley below. Its stone walls, battlements and towers, dominated the landscape as it leered up at them. Gwen realized that she was trembling. Upon their arrival they were ordered to make camp outside the walls and were told that they were expected to perform the following evening, when the King was due back from a hunting trip.

The well dressed gentleman greeted them and politely thanked them for coming. He instructed where in the great hall they should perform and told them that their performance was to mark a great and important occasion. A truce had been agreed. After years of conflict, the Danish King from the North was to be a special guest and the feast was being prepared in his honour. Brendan gulped.

That afternoon, they prepared for the performance of their lives. There were many trips back and forth from their little camp as they set up their stage before massive oak tables in the cavernous hall. It was during these frantic comings and goings that the hunting party returned. The minstrels' anxiety grew as they found themselves mutely staring at the incoming procession of fur clad men who bristled with bows and spears as they lumbered past on their heavy, snorting horses. The Captain shrunk back into the darkness of a wagon, his eyes growing large at the sound of the yelping, thick-necked stocky dogs that obediently trailed behind their masters. In their midst, trundled a flat wagon. Upon it, with glassy eyes and lolling tongues, were piled butchered stags from the hunt.

---

[*] Edward I the Elder. Eldest son of Alfred the Great and King of the Anglo-Saxons (899-924).

Afternoon forced the sun lower in the sky and their preparations at last were complete. The time of the performance was finally upon them. Both the Captain and Artus sensed the fear in their friends. With trembling fingers the minstrels dressed in their bright costumes and left their friendly little camp. They felt small as they entered the huge door of the castle.

"We'll give 'em a show they'll remember," said Brendan bravely in a higher voice than was usual. The others agreed with theatrical enthusiasm as their voices echoed amid the cold stone and they passed beneath the teeth of the portcullis. Illuminated by flaming torches, they made their way to the great hall where the well dressed gentleman waited for them at the heavy oaken door. His superior calm had been replaced with servile fluster. Beyond, they could hear thunderous bursts of laughter, shouts and yells. "Are you ready?" asked the gentleman in a hoarse voice that suggested that perhaps he was not.

"As ready as we'll ever be," replied Brendan with a wry smile to his friends. The great door was thrown open and in they danced and skipped as they played their instruments with Gwen singing and Artus dancing to rowdy cheers and the rhythmic pounding of cup and fist on wood. Now, seated behind the heavy tables, were the lords and ladies of many powerful Saxon households. At their centre sat King Edward, and at his side, King Eohric of the Vikings of East Anglia.

"My King, honoured guests, Lords, Ladies and Gentlemen. It is our great pleasure to introduce Artus, the last bear in Britain!"

Artus danced, the minstrels played, and to the thundering of hands on table, the bear gave a deep royal bow. The performance continued with ballads (one written especially for the occasion, perhaps unimaginatively entitled "Edward, King of the Angles and Saxons, what more is left to say?") There was song, juggling, and fire-eating (interrupted amid much mirth by an enthusiastic dousing of pungent wine from the Vikings). There was near suicidal stilt-walking as one stilt accidently skated upon a discarded chicken carcass in a large harrowing arc, bringing a loud cheer from the boisterous and appreciative audience. Given the vertical distances involved and their tenuous apex, excruciating injury was but narrowly avoided.

At last it was time for the final performance with Brendan and the Captain. Behind the curtain, Brendan placed the Captain on his wizard table and kissed him on the head. The Captain noticed the uncharacteristic beads of sweat that gleamed on Brendan's forehead.

"Just stick to the script and we'll be fine," whispered Brendan. The Captain nodded his reassurance. They heard beyond the curtain:

"And now, from the depths of time and direct from the magical Otherworld of Annwn, we bring you Merlin and his familiar!"

The curtain was swept aside and there stood Brendan with his arms aloft. The audience leaned forward in unusually quiet study. A woman giggled somewhere.

"Behold!" cried Merlin in his wavering wizard voice. "Behold, my spirit guide as ancient as the Druids. Together, we will amaze and confound you!"

There was a pause and Brendan looked at the Captain who seemed to be lost in thought.

"Amaze and confound!" cried Brendan loudly, dramatically opening his eyes wide and peering about the room. Again, he looked at the Captain and swept close to him.

"What's wrong?" he whispered hoarsely.

"Sorry, I remember something. Leaf."

"Never mind now, keep to the script." Merlin opened his arms and cried out again,

"Amaze…and…confound."

The Captain peered about the room and the audience leaned in closer. "We will amaze and confound you!" he called out in his theatrical voice.

Brendan heaved such a sigh of relief that he forgot to move his beard in the manner of a ventriloquist. Members of the esteemed audience began whispering amongst themselves.

"In days gone by when magic flowed as from an enchanted spring in the garden of Britain," quavered Brendan regaining their attention, "wizards and their familiars wielded power beyond imagination. I will now connect with the ancients." He closed his eyes and the Captain spoke:

"We are the ancient ones of Britain," (Brendan, back in his stride was twitching the beard to plan) "and we say all hail to the King."

There was raucous applause and cheers throughout the room and the King was smiling benevolently. Beside him, the Danish King was whispering close in his ear. Brendan was about to continue the act but the King stood up. Everyone became quiet.

"We had word that you owned this last bear of our kingdom. It has been many years since we have had opportunity to hunt such a beast. Our cousin, King Eohric, being long now upon these shores and missing this great sport of home is happy that you are here. I will purchase your bear in the spirit of our friendship. We will make sport of him with our dogs following the feast and all are invited to the spectacle."

A deafening yell went up. The King sat down and he and Eohric tapped their cups together. Slowly the tumult eased.

"Pray continue," said the King, casually leaning on the arm of his chair.

The Captain looked at Brendan who stood with his mouth half open in a look of abject horror. He turned and could see the other minstrels to the rear and at one side of the stage. There, Artus sat quietly and patiently as was his manner. He saw tears rolling down Gwen's cheek. Her lips were tightly pressed together; her shoulders shaking. The room seemed suddenly to be out of focus and the Captain saw colours in his mind. He saw a round house in a clearing and felt the gentle touch of an old man's hand upon his head.

"There is no need for payment for the bear," the Captain called out to the King. Brendan, though still in shock, remembered to move the beard but looked desperately at the Captain who was saying, "Instead, we would like to offer a challenge."

The King's smile faded. "A challenge?" he repeated with a frown.

Brendan's beard twitched maniacally.

"We have one final illusion to perform for your pleasure," the Captain continued. "If you, or any member of the company, are able to discern how this illusion is created, then you shall have our bear. If, however, you are unable to discover the secret of it, then in the spirit of the evening, the bear is forfeit to you."

The King whispered with his Danish visitor and turned. "Show us this illusion of which you speak. If it shall impress us then you shall keep the bear and our sport shall be cancelled."

As the perspiration now dripped from his face, Brendan was staring at the Captain with frightened wide eyes.

"Minstrels play and Artus dance," commanded the Captain.

There was a pause and then a fumbling for instruments. A familiar theme was struck up. Artus happily came forward once more and he began to dance. The bear took centre stage between the tables and began to hop from one foot to the other.

Brendan leaned close to the Captain. "What is going on?" he rasped.

"I remember," said the Captain. He closed his eyes tightly and the music dissolved. His ears were ringing. A deep pool. A hand to cling too. A face close to his. He could see the forest glade where an old man stood holding his staff high in the air with eyes clenched shut in concentration and connection, head thrown back, coming into focus, he laughed and struck at the ground.

The Captain was staring into blinding light. He was filled with breath. "You are free!" he shouted.

There was a clatter of metal. All that remained of Artus were his chains upon the floor.

The great hall was silent. Brendan looked at Gwen. Gwen looked at the Captain. Everyone looked at each other. King Eohric stood and opened his arms, a big grin on his face.

"You do confound and amaze us. You win the challenge," he boomed and the hall was filled again with applause and cheers.

The door was opened and with utter confusion written upon his face, the finely dressed but increasingly dishevelled gentleman stood aside to let Artus lumber back into the room. The bear stood and made his bow.

"This has been a most excellent entertainment. I invite you to our house at East Angle."

"You honour us, sir," said Brendan who turned to the Captain and kissed him on the head.

Shortly after their Royal command performance, the little group retreated across the English Channel to Brittany, having tired, very quickly, of the strains of the big time. Here, they travelled the country lanes in their wagons and their many talents were celebrated in the towns and village squares where they performed. Merlin and his familiar, however, were conspicuously absent, for fear of attracting too much celebrity status. Prudently, ventriloquism was not mentioned again.

THE LIGHTNING TREE

It was a cold March in the year 1140. The snows of winter still clung tenuously to the land. It lay sheltered by hedgerows, gleaming in the shadows. Spring seemed unwilling to disturb the long winter, as though the land was enchanted, held in time, barely awake. The stillness belied the devastation that civil war had wrought in the land.[*] The towns and cities had become armed camps and the countryside a lawless and dangerous place, where bands of brigands and robber barons answered to no law and where honest people lived in great fear. Villages and houses had been pillaged and burned, thousands had been displaced.

Light snow fell now in the crisp morning as the Captain journeyed through the forest. He blinked as the flakes attached themselves to his whiskers. He travelled in a thick carpet bag which Hugh de Paynes wore as usual across his back. Together, they had been scorched in the heat at Antioch where they had battled swift riding cavalry, scimitars gleaming in the sun. For twelve years they had protected pilgrims on the long road to Jerusalem where they had endured aching famine and constant skirmishes. But the years of battle had taken their toll and Hugh had become weary of fighting. His tanned face was heavily lined, his hair and beard shot with grey as he had prepared their camp at the ruin of the Temple of Solomon. He had lain down and stroked the Captain's thick fur. And under the velvet eastern sky, he dreamed of a tree:

He was standing in light snow, looking up at a hill in the chill

---

[*] Civil war between the supporters of Stephen of Blois, King of England 1135-54 (grandson of William the Conqueror) and Matilda (daughter of Henry I).

evening. A huge oak tree stood at the top of the hill illuminated by the bright moon. The shadow of the giant with its uplifted limbs and myriad fingers fell across the landscape so that the hillside became a silken tapestry picked out in glowing beams of moonlight. Although it was winter in the dream, the great tree was covered in leaves that shimmered and whispered together though no breeze was felt. In his dream, Hugh was drawn towards the tree. Walking across the moonlit carpet, the leaves whispered to him and he strained his ears to hear. Looking around him at the hill on which he stood, he saw the night sky reflected in every detail so that the tree was at the centre of the universe and the beauty and mystery of it took his breath away.

He awoke in the warm Jerusalem evening still smelling the crisp air of the dream, the tang of woodland in his nostrils, and with the conviction that the place in his dream was real and that he must seek it out.

So it was that the knight and his cat began their journey in search of the tree. Trusting in faith and intuition, they travelled north, back along the pilgrim road and across the sea to Albion.[*] The desert sands were now replaced by icy ponds, gurgling brooks and green forests.

It had been days since they had seen a living soul and Hugh was anxious to ask if such a tree was known. It was with a sense of relief then, that as they made their way out of the forest into open country, they saw a thin wisp of smoke in the distance. They made their way towards it across long neglected fields, and late in the afternoon came upon a small village of grey stone houses. Hugh nudged his horse on and approached two ragged children playing with ice from the well. He hailed them but they turned screaming into a house. A man came running, wielding an axe. With wide eyes he stared at Hugh and yelled to the children to stay inside. Hugh held up a supplicant hand.

"My deepest apologies sir, I didn't mean to frighten the children," he said.

The man stared at him suspiciously, but he relaxed his grip on the axe. "They would be thinking you were Resquillier."

"Resquillier?"

---

[*] Britain or England (Old English via Latin from Celtic)

"Williem de Resquillier, one of your Norman brothers who terrifies the country here and who has robbed us of all that we had so that there is nothing to seed the fields."

"You are mistaken, brother," said Hugh, "for I hail from Anjou and am come recently from the Holy land. This Resquillier I know not."

"Then you are lucky...brother." The farmer spat out the last word with contempt before he turned and walked back to the house. Hugh shrugged and asked his horse to walk on.

The man slowed his step, stopped and turned. "Wait," he called. "Resquillier may have taken all else but he has not stolen my humanity. It will be dark soon, shelter here by all means. We have little but you are welcome to share what we have."

Hugh thanked him and dismounted.

With his horse fed, watered and safely stabled under a dry lean-to, Hugh sat down with the family in their small smoky cottage as the Captain curled himself in a warm corner. Their supper was rabbit stew and Hugh sipped gratefully as the children watched in silent scrutiny. He asked the man, whose name was Gyric, if he knew of the existence of a great oak tree. Gyric narrowed his eyes as he answered. "You are the second stranger in as many days to ask about the tree."

"Indeed?" said Hugh raising his eyebrows.

"The children met her out in the field and she asked directions for the Lightning Tree."

Hugh stopped eating and sat back. "The Lightning Tree?"

"An oak tree of great age and girth which sits upon a hill not three days north along the Roman road. It is well known and impossible to miss. Many tales have attached themselves to it and the hill itself is said to be a burial place of the ancients."

"And you say a woman was asking after it?"

Gyric looked at his young son and gestured with a nod of his head. The boy looked shy and whispered so that Hugh strained to hear. "She had black skin, was wrapped in a cloak and riding a horse quite as great as yours. She asked us what was the most noble tree that we knew of and we told her about the Lightning Tree. Then she gave us the coin and rode away. When she turned we saw that on her back was a round shield with a picture of a tree upon it."

"What coin is this?" demanded Gyric. "You did not mention a coin!"

The child looked sheepish and feeling within the folds of his ragged smock he laid a coin in his father's hand. Gyric frowned, turning it over. "I've not seen the like," he said and passed it to the knight who held it in the light of the single candle.

"It looks to be very old," said Hugh, "perhaps Egyptian. Here is your seed money. It is gold, of that I am sure," He handed the coin back to Gyric as the children sat open-mouthed.

The following morning, the children guided Hugh and the Captain to the place where they had met the strange woman. There, though softened by the new fallen snow, he found the tracks of her horse. He thanked the children and judging Gyric to be too proud to accept it, he made his own contribution of seed money to them. They thanked him with serious faces, then, to the harsh cry of the crows that jostled each other in the nearby trees, he struck out for the north, following in the tracks of the woman, the Captain peering over Hugh's shoulder from the safety of the carpet bag.

It was easy going over open country and rested, the knight's horse made good progress as they cantered on through the frosty morning. At noon they arrived at a small copse. The sun was a pale smudge behind a blanket of cloud. All colour seemed to have drained from the world. Within the copse he found a camp site where he guessed the woman had rested for the night— the fire cinders were still warm at their centre. However, there were other tracks now which suggested a dozen or so more horses. Amid the chaos of the churned ground, Hugh was able to discern the tracks of the woman leaving the copse at a leisurely pace but these new fresher tracks were made by horses spurred to a gallop. He concluded that she was being followed and regaining his mount, he too began his pursuit in earnest.

It had been a deep curiosity which had compelled him to follow the tracks of the stranger, but his curiosity had grown into concern. He sensed danger.

Baron Williem de Resquillier's grandfather had invaded Britain with the Conqueror in 1066.[*] In payment for his service he had been awarded land in the north of England—land which his grandson now presided over with brutal effect. In a kingdom devoid of governance he filled the vacuum with a cruel relish. He demanded that the people of his little realm be effectively enslaved to him and what was not given he stole, whether it be food, money or property. If there was any protest he would murder entire families, burn entire villages. On this day he was out for sport, hunting with his bully-boy friends and henchmen. Their sport had become a chase for the fun of it when they found the camp fire in the copse. They would relieve someone of their horse (for trespassing) and of their purse and any other precious thing they may have (for a fine). If there was resistance they would execute their own justice. And so they pounded on across the icy landscape until at last they spied their quarry in the distance—a single rider, an easy target.

Resquillier had taken pleasure in hanging "witches" in the past, spurred on by the superstitions and fears of those he controlled. These victims were usually old women who made a poor living by selling ointments and cures. This then, was Resquillier's world, but he was not worldly. Not wise. If he had been so he might have exercised more caution, would have taken more care, for the stranger that he now pursued was not a poor serf, nor an old woman who sold ointments for rheumatism. This stranger was the real thing. This stranger was the Witch of Nu from the land of ancient Abyssinia and now she turned her darkening eyes upon her pursuers.

It was a short time later that the noble Hugh reined in his horse at the sight of Norman riders, scattered, and riding back towards him. They paid him no heed as they raggedly rode past at speed, but he noticed well the look of terror on their faces. He drew his sword and moved on cautiously. Following the tracks, he came to a small icy hollow hemmed in by a dark wood.

Here lay the bodies of three Norman soldiers, their blood vivid and fresh upon the frozen ground.

Hugh's horse snorted with nervous dips of its head, prancing

---

[*] William the Conqueror, Duke of Normandy, defeated King Harold of the Anglo-Saxons at the battle of Hastings in 1066 and claimed the English throne.

sideways in the ice. Hugh's grip tightened on his sword as he glanced about him, sensing the danger, and suddenly she was there, riding at a walk out of the dark wood; fixing him with her calm stare, her cloak thrown back to reveal a suit of mail and glinting breastplate. In her hand shimmered a long claw-like blade and at her shoulder was a round shield that bore the image of a tree.

Hugh sensed her power; his long experience held no match; her malevolence was palpable as she moved closer. His heart pounded as he steeled himself for he knew not what and then suddenly, she stopped. She seemed unsure or was it… yes, curiosity, and Hugh realized that she was staring at his cat.

The Captain had climbed out of his carpet bag and now curled himself around Hugh's shoulder. He blinked at the witch. He was not afraid. In her he sensed a friend.

"Why do you come here, knight?" she asked in a quiet voice.

"I saw the tracks at your camp site," Hugh answered. "There is one Resquillier who I know is afoot in the country, I followed in the belief that he meant harm."

Her expression didn't change as she spoke again. "I need not your protection, Crusader. Now answer well. Why do you come here?"

Her eyes were fixed on his now as she moved forward again. Hugh held her stare, remembering that they shared a quest. With a dry mouth he said, "I dreamed of a magical tree that revealed the universe to me. I am come to find it. To find if it is real."

The smile was unexpected and broke upon her face as the warm sun will transform a dark and brooding landscape. As she smoothly swung her sword into its scabbard upon her back she patted her horse and said, "It is the living ancestor. It is real. Follow me knight, for time presses—the moon is on the wane."

So it was that Hugh and the Captain now joined company with the Witch of Nu and they set off together in search of the tree. They rode in silence across the sleeping landscape, the horses' footfalls muffled in the new snow. Hugh was burning with curiosity; was filled with questions, but the awe in which he held his companion made him thoughtful and quiet. He allowed himself furtive glances as she walked ahead. Her immaculate appearance seemed to him to be somehow unreal. Scorched into his memory was her advance on him from the dark wood at the hollow. The fear that had gripped his soldier's heart still disconcerted him.

They continued in silence throughout the afternoon, and as the sun began to dip below the horizon, the snow began to fall with greater intensity. They came upon a small burned out church. The witch turned in her saddle. "We are close now. It will be a black and moonless night. We will rest our horses here."

With that she swung herself to the ground and led her horse through the open door of the church. Hugh stretched his back and dismounted. Peering northward through the flurries of snow he glimpsed a hill in the distance, upon it the dark shape of a great tree. It was there and then gone as the light quickly faded and he was enveloped in cold darkness. He too led his horse inside. Impossibly, a fire had been kindled within the devastated nave. The woman had removed her saddle and was brushing her horse close by. Hugh eased the saddle from his own mount and looking around at the little church he saw that the altar was still intact; a wooden cross still stood there. He knelt, crossed himself and said a silent prayer.

Resquillier had bolted under the onslaught at the hollow and had ridden at speed for his slit-eyed keep. He had paced up and down in his chamber. He had tried to make sense of what he had seen. Who was the dark warrior? He had ordered out his garrison of fifty mounted cavalry. They had wasted no time, had swept across the country kicking in doors, demanding information about a black woman on a horse. Nothing, no sign, not until his henchman Coup-Jarret arrived at Gyric's house. Gyric had resisted and was beaten until the children cried out what they knew, cried out the name of the Lightning Tree. Within hours, the Norman cavalry was thundering north along the Roman road.

Somewhere in the distance, strangely muffled in the falling snow, wolves were howling for the invisible moon. Inside the little church, the fractured walls danced with shadows from the leaping fire. On one side of the flames sat the knight with his cat, on the other, sat the witch. Hugh had offered her dry biscuit which she had declined politely, surprising him by thanking him for the thought. He watched her now across the fire as she sat with eyes closed, her back straight, her face a mask of chiselled ebony. Then she was looking back—for a moment the eyes terrifying, black as bottomless pits as they had been at the hollow—then they softened, became human. Green eyes. "Tell me about your dream."

The inquiry was posed gently and with sincerity so that Hugh relaxed. He told her about the hill, the oak tree in the moonlight and the whispering leaves.

She nodded slowly. "Tell me about the cat."

Hugh was perplexed and he glanced down at the Captain who was sleeping in his lap. Looking at his cat, he sighed and described how they had always travelled together, how invaluable was their companionship and how the Captain seemed to know what he was saying. He was smiling as he talked, stroking the Captain's thick fur.

The Captain stirred and arched his back as he stretched and sat looking at the witch. She was holding a small wooden box which she rested in the palm of her left hand. With a touch of her finger, its lid opened and reverently she lifted from it, by its narrow stem, a golden oak leaf which she held in the air.

The Captain watched, transfixed, as the leaf shimmered in the light of the fire. The words came to him with a shocking jolt and Hugh felt the Captain spasm. He held the cat defensively. Sound was sucked from the air, the fire crackled in silence and diminished so that the church became dark. Only the leaf was glowing in the air. Hugh sensed others around them, they whispered now and a voice was crying out, "Leaf, leaf, leaf."

There was a click as the lid of the box closed in the witches' palm, the leaf returned within it. The fire resumed. Hugh looked at the Captain who blinked back at him with unconcern and then at the witch who sat with her eyes closed again, a contented smile on her face as she drew a deep breath and sighed. Hugh felt confused and suddenly angry. "Who are you?" he snapped.

Her green eyes opened. "I am Nu and this leaf was brought to me by the Followers. Tomorrow we will come to the tree that bore it and we shall see what we shall see. Sleep now Hugh de Paynes. You are a good man and have nothing to fear from me."

She closed her eyes and said no more. Hugh stepped out into the night. Even in the blackness he could just see that the only tracks into the church belonged to himself and the witch. He had thought there had been others. He had thought he had heard them. He listened now but could only hear the blood pounding in his ears. The land was silent. He returned and wrapped himself in his cloak, eventually falling asleep propped against the wall, his hand resting on the hilt of his sword.

He awoke with a shiver as dawn glowed in the windows of the little church. Wrapped in his cloak, he stumbled past the horses and looked outside. There she was, kneeling in the snow, the Captain watching her. Without looking around she spoke to Hugh. "The dark moon is reborn and is rising with the sun. She cannot be seen but she is there. We follow."

The sun broke upon the horizon revealing a bright clear sky, and there in the distance stood the hill, upon it, the great dark mass of the tree. They mounted their horses and with care made their way through the fresh snow, the Captain tucked up in his carpet bag. Hugh was heartened by the warmth of the sun on his face but unease lingered within him. He had made his journey, however, and the object of his quest lay before him. He would see it through. As the sun rose higher in the sky, the tree grew larger as they made their way towards it. Their breath formed clouds in the air. *At least she breathes*, thought Hugh, *if she breathes she is human.*

In time they drew close to the base of the hill and looked up at the Lightning Tree which stood like a mute giant in the landscape. Its roots still held the earth in a giant's grip; its body still cast a giant's shadow. Its strickened limbs seemed still to be racked by the violence of the ancient tree's electrocution, held for all time in twisted anguish, held up towards heaven in defiance of its scorched fate.

Hugh looked uncertain as he dismounted and glanced towards the witch. Her brow was creased in a frown. "The tree is dead," said Hugh with a sigh. "We're too late."

They stood gazing up at the dead hulk on the hill and the silence was broken by yells in the distance. Hugh turned and saw the line of fifty Norman cavalry riding towards them through the snow.

"Resquillier," he said under his breath and looked back to the witch who was now walking up the hill towards the tree. "We must go. Now," he shouted.

She didn't seem to hear him. He ran through the snow after her and grabbed her shoulder, spinning her round. Her green eyes were glistening, tears like diamonds shone upon her cheeks. He was stunned into a moment's silence. "We must go," he said softly. "It is over."

"Will you trust me, knight?" she said quietly.

He looked back towards Resquillier and his cavalry, now but moments from the hill. He shrugged. These were impossible odds anyway and it was now too late to outride them.

"Very well," he said as the Captain curled himself around his shoulder. "Very well."

She smiled and taking his hand she led him towards the tree. Two hundred and thirty-eight yards away, Resquillier gave the order to draw swords and advance. Two hundred and thirty-eight thousand miles away, the silent moon was reaching its invisible zenith in the sky. The noon sun now beamed directly over the tree as the witch held out her hand and touched its iron bark. The moon continued upon its course and moved between the earth and the sun. The land grew dark as the eclipse cast its shadow upon it and night replaced the day again.[*]

Hugh watched as Resquillier's cavalry scattered, the horses panicking, their riders terrified. He looked at the witch and together they turned their eyes to the heavens, to the black sun that glowed in the sky, and above them a whispering canopy of golden leaves appeared upon the branches sending beams of golden light dancing and revolving like stars around them.

"Leaf," said the Captain. "Leaf, leaf, leaf."

Hugh was stunned into silence but the witch was smiling at him. A gentle smile, perhaps tinged with pity. "Cat got your tongue?" she whispered.

Hugh looked blank.

"Gentle knight, it was not your dream that you remembered. It was his."

---

[*] A total solar eclipse occurred on March 20, 1140 and is recorded in the *Anglo Saxon Chronicle.*

The Captain had leapt to the ground and now climbed into the branches of the great tree, the leaves whispering around him. There among the bifurcation of limbs where the lightning had struck, was a hole, and the Captain climbed down into it. He was in a dark wooden hall of enormous proportion and as the moon moved through the sky it released the first rays of the sun and the hall was filled with light. A thousand silver disks shone around him and he descended deeper, deeper into the hill. The Followers lit the way now through stone passageways and the Captain followed, knowing them for friends. They spoke in whispers. "He's here, he's here, he's here."

The Captain whispered back, "I'm here, I'm here."

"And so you are, my little friend."

The voice was familiar—and then the Captain saw him. Like a vision, but very real, the Druid of Môn was glowing brightly in the darkness and smiling his old smile.

The Captain cried as the memories flooded back to him of their little house in the forest. He leapt up and was enfolded in gentle arms. "We're together again!" he said, nuzzling the old man.

"For a short time my little friend, until the sun is whole. Then you must return to the world and to your noble friends who wait upon you even as we speak."

"But I will see you again?"

The old man smiled again. "When the journeys are done. When the mysteries are revealed. When it is time." He slipped a small pouch around the Captain's neck. "Take this to the Witch of Nu. She has made a long journey at our request and she knows what to do."

"I love you," said the Captain.

The old man hugged him. "I love you too."

The Followers were whispering, "Time to go, time to go, time to go."

The old man hugged the Captain again. "Quickly, my little friend. For now our time is fleeting but I will be here when you return."

The Followers beckoned and the Captain was whisked back along the passages and up, up, up into the light where finches and sparrows sang their morning chorus. As the bright leaves slowly faded, Hugh and the witch were watching as the Captain reappeared. He blinked at them as the crisp air filled his lungs and the last slim crescent of moon shadow melted from the face of the sun. He stood in the derelict branches of the blackened Lightning Tree as the illuminated beauty of the world surrounded him.

THE CATHEDRAL CLOCK

In 1482, at the centre of life, was a palace of megalithic limestone; an ordered symmetry of towers and flying buttresses, of chapels and tracery, which the Captain called his home. He was the cathedral cat.

He had been born with four brothers and sisters in a corner of the stonemason's workshop on a bright midsummer's day. For the following twelve years, wearing his sleek coat of clerical black and white, it had been his duty to patrol with austerity and keep the mice and rats at bay.

His home was very old and very large indeed. Its great vaulted ceiling supported on massive stone pillars seemed to the Captain like a forest glade of towering oak trees, their impressive branches intertwining to block out the sky. With satisfaction, he would climb the worn steps of the Norman towers and look out over the bustling city and market place which congregated about the great church as planets congregate about their sun and are held there with unquestioning gravity. Often, he would visit his sisters at the Bishop's Palace. Here, they would sit curled together in front of the blazing fire and blink and blink again. By evening, the Captain would always return to the cathedral to see to his duties, for it was at night that he took custody of his charge.[*] He would wander the silent expanse of the nave or explore the labyrinth of wooden tracery in the quire. Nonchalantly, he would wash his paws as he sat upon the cool chest of the prone Bishop Stapeldon, whose marble effigy lay for all time in prayer, his feet resting upon a snarling marble lion.

---

[*] Medieval accounts in the archives at Exeter Cathedral in Devon record that the cathedral cat was considered a member of the cathedral staff and received payment of one penny per week.

During the day, the Captain relaxed and could often be found curled up in a golden sunbeam at the end of a bench beneath Saint Michael who was made of glass and glowed in the sky. During services, he would often sit silently and unseen in the minstrel's gallery and look down upon the clerics, clergy, pilgrims and public. He would listen to their echoed words and share in their communion. He found comfort in the stability and the repetition; in the events and services which recurred with the regularity of the seasons, as inevitably as night follows the day.

The cathedral cat knew every inch of his territory inside and out, from the great west door to the Lady Chapel, from the highest battlement to the depths of the crypt. But of all the many chapels, cloisters, flags and windows, the altars, paintings, galleries and bosses there was one thing that held the Captain's interest more than anything. It was an interest inspired by the notion of measuring time and made manifest by the great predictor, the heartbeat, the axis around which all revolved: the cathedral clock. It served to allow the bells to be rung at regular intervals which would improve productivity in the city it was said, so that once installed, it became the means to measure the industry of men.

The clock lived in the north wall of the north tower, tucked in by the Chapel of the Holy Cross and facing out into the quire. Upon its large, blue face were three concentric rings mounted with symbols arranged around a glittering golden orb. Around the orb, within the rings, very slowly, moved a silver disk. To one side of the clock was a small wooden door which led to the giant mechanism which drove the silver disk. At the base of the door, a hole had been cut by the carpenter, allowing the Captain access to prevent mice and rats from nesting in or damaging the delicate machinery. The Captain would sit for hours inside the door watching the great metal wheels slowly revolve with an escapement of tick, tick, tick.

Several years before, the Captain had learned how to predict events by looking at where the silver disk was, as it travelled its daily journey around the giant circle of the clock. By studying the movement, he knew which window the sun would be shining through; when the bell-ringers would haul on the sally of their ropes; when services would begin, or when his friend the Bishop would arrive. After years of this study, there was one event which still terrified and fascinated him. It occurred every year on the same day: it was the appearance of the lady in black.

The Captain always knew it was time for the lady in black by the nature of the service which preceded her. It was unusual because it was the only service to be held in the middle of the winter in the middle of the night. Many people would crowd into the big house for this service, and the minstrel's gallery would be filled with musicians. The Captain would perch on the north transept balcony and look down at the flickering candles and the thronging crowd who came to sing and pray. When the service was over, the people would drift away in a burble of conversation and the Verger would make his rounds as he whistled absentmindedly through his teeth. Then, he too would leave, locking the door behind him with a hollow clank and the Captain would find himself quite alone.

At this time, he would march straight to the clock and wait patiently until the silver disk was pointing to an angel on the transept ceiling. This was the signal for him to scuttle back to the nave, hide himself away, and watch the piece of wall beneath the regimental plaque in readiness for the event.

As the moment approached he felt his skin begin to tingle and his eyes would grow dark. His fur would stand on end as he shrank back into the shadows. There, in front of him, a thickening mist would form in the bruised air like a threat, as silent as a thunder cloud before a violent storm. Identical, year in and year out, the cloud would blacken to the colour of dense charcoal and compress itself into the stark figure of the lady in black. Stepping from the wall, she would stand motionless for a moment, turning her pale face left and right. Then, she would glide into the cathedral and the Captain's fur would bristle as the air grew cold.

After twelve years, the familiarity and repetition of the event allowed the Captain to control the panic that gripped him in this moment. Fear had been replaced by curiosity and adventure, so that instead of hiding as he had done in the past, the Captain became determined to follow the lady in black. She first glided towards the quire. The Captain followed her keeping his body low to the ground and moved swiftly from shadow to shadow. She stopped when she arrived at the High Altar and knelt. The Captain strained his ears as he watched and could hear her whispering with frantic speed. Then, there blurted a profound sob which shocked him with its echo. She rose to her feet and made her rapid journey to the door of the north tower. The Captain watched as the lady passed through the solid door. He followed at a trot and went through the little hole that the carpenter had cut for him to guard the clock, he then watched as the lady began to glide up the narrow, dark, stone staircase. Higher and higher she climbed with the Captain running in her icy wake. At last, she arrived at the very top, paused by the great bell, and then passed through the door onto the tower roof. The Captain looked around for some way to follow her but the door was shut fast and offered the only means of access to the roof. He pressed his ear to the door but could only hear the wind.

The Captain was left standing alone and awash with an overwhelming feeling of sadness. He was disappointed that he had been unable to follow the lady but the sadness was something he could not explain. It lingered in the air like a tear-stain and then quietly faded away.

The cathedral cat determined to continue with his duties and to wait another year.

The year passed much as the proceeding years had passed. There were trips to the Bishop's Palace to visit his sisters; afternoons curled up in the summer sunshine, and always the fascination of the cathedral clock, as the silver disk imperceptibly followed its inevitable journey around the golden orb, day after day, night after night.

The year was also spent in planning and preparation for the next midwinter night and the visit of the lady. The Captain first found a spot beneath the giant High Altar, where he would be able to conceal himself within feet of the lady when she knelt there. He found a space behind the tracery where he could watch and more importantly, listen, without disturbing the ritual. There were also trips to the north tower. Apart from the door, the only access to the tower roof was a slit of a window high in the wall. Again and again, the Captain practiced leaping to the ledge. In time, and with experience, he found deformities and erosions in the wall which allowed him to find purchase. Instead of leaping directly toward the little window, he would leap from one side to the other, onto a narrow ledge, then to the corner where the stone was angled. Finally, he was able to use his momentum to land upon the little window ledge itself, where he was afforded a clear and unobstructed view out onto the roof.

Summer waned and autumn nipped at the world outside. Trees were beginning their hibernation, and birds their migration as the solar wheel turned in the sky. The Captain watched the leaves turning to shades of russet and brown in the cathedral close. The nights grew longer and darker as winter arrived with a chill sigh; the branches of the trees became bare and soon they were laden with snow.

The year had come full circle as the night of the Midnight Mass arrived and the cathedral was filled once more with hosts of people and with the familiar music and words of the special night. The minstrel's gallery was filled with musicians again and the Captain perched on the north transept balcony looking down at the glow of candles and the crowd. The service ended, the Verger made his whistling rounds and patted the Captain on the head as he passed. He left and locked the door behind him and the Captain was again alone.

The heavy silence seemed all the more palpable with the departure of the bustling congregation. With darkening eyes he waited in front of the clock. The silver disk edged along on its certain journey and the angel on the transept roof stared down with muted prophesy. When finally, finally, the two were aligned, the Captain moved into his position out of sight in the nave and waited with pounding heart for the return of the lady in black.

As had been the case the year before and for many years before that, the cathedral began to grow cold. The Captain felt his skin begin to tingle, his fur to stand on end. Beneath the regimental plaque a thickening, dark cloud was forming. The Captain raced to his planned hiding place beneath the altar. His large dark eyes looked out from between the curling stone tracery. He felt himself shivering as out of the gloom toward him, silently, glided the lady in black. As she came closer and closer, the Captain struggled against the strong instinct to run. She came within feet of him so that in her close proximity he felt the numbing, icy air, more powerfully than he had ever experienced it. She knelt and was level with his vantage point. He held his breath as her white face seemed to float and flicker before him like a cold candle flame. Her pale eyes were unblinking as her lips began to form words. She spoke with rasping frenzy.

"Forgive me, forgive me, forgive me. My sin will never be washed away. Never washed away and my heart is broken. Forgive me for what I have done and for what I am about to do. I will never rest while we are parted because he cannot rest. Never rest. For I have buried him and cannot confess it to anyone but you. Please help me. Please let him rest in peace."

The sob that followed was a blast of raw remorse. As the lady stood, the Captain found it hard to watch her stricken face. She turned and moved towards the north tower. The Captain swallowed, left his hiding place, and raced through his hole in the door. Up and up the tower staircase he climbed while just ahead of him, turning the corner on every stair flight, was the silent and icy figure of the lady in black. At last she arrived at the top, paused at the bell, and disappeared through the closed door. With heart pounding the Captain leapt, just as he had practiced, and found the vantage point overlooking the roof. There, he saw the lady standing on the edge, balanced upon the rampart. She opened her arms wide and as the Captain cried out helplessly, she launched herself into the void.

Over the next few days, the Captain decided to make sense of the mystery. He began by examining the area beneath the tower in the Cathedral Green. Looking up, he could gauge where the lady had stood on the rampart. To his excitement, he found half buried and obscured by grass, a cracked stone tablet bearing an inscription and a weathered image of a nun kneeling in prayer. Next, the Captain studied the wall beneath the regimental plaque where the lady always appeared. It seemed as uniform as the wall that surrounded it, but the Captain was convinced that the answer to the puzzle lay here.

Now, in 1482, if a cat uttered a word to anybody, let alone confided a story of mysterious and ghostly nuns he was sure at the very least, to be deemed unfit for cathedral duties. It was with trepidation then, that he left the cathedral one night and made his way to the Bishop's Palace where he hid in a cupboard of the Bishop's bed chamber. He watched through a crack in the door as the Bishop prepared for bed and then waited for him to fall asleep. After several hours he scratched at the door, louder and louder, until he heard the Bishop stir.

"Fear not," cried the Captain in what he hoped was a solemn and otherworldly voice. He heard the Bishop gasp and saw him sit bolt upright in the dark.

"Fear not," he said again.

"Who's there?" asked the Bishop in an uncertain voice.

"I speak to you in a dream," said the Captain. "Only you can lay my poor soul to rest."

The Captain saw that the Bishop was clasping his hands together in prayer.

"What...what do you ask of me?" said the Bishop.

"Look beneath the north tower and you will know me from a stone tablet buried there. Look beneath the regimental memorial and you will discover my secret." The Captain allowed his voice to trail away with dramatic effect, an ancient memory of minstrels glowing brightly in his mind. The Bishop remained sitting up in bed for some time in prayer, but finally he settled back and drifted off to sleep. The Captain quietly slipped out of the room and returned to the cathedral.

The next morning's flurry of activity surprised even the Captain. The Bishop arrived earlier than usual, trailing a gaggle of his Deans and Clergy. Prayers were uttered constantly. The Captain followed the crowd as they moved outside and began to search the ground beneath the north tower. They looked everywhere but in the right place so that the Captain was forced to attract the attention of the Verger by scratching at the ground. The Verger wondered over and kicked at the ground with his toe. Finding the stone he yelped and the crowd gathered around them. The throngs parted like the biblical Red Sea as the Bishop arrived and knelt at the stone. The Captain stayed close by and listened as the Bishop read aloud, "'Here is the place where our beloved sister fell from the tower. God rest her soul.' It is very old," remarked the Bishop. There was general muttering and more whispered prayers. The Bishop pointed towards the cathedral with great drama. "The second part of my vision concerns the nave," he said, and with great importance he swept off in his flowing robes followed by his whispering retinue, the Captain trailing in their wake.

Inside the nave, the stonemason was waiting with his tools laid out on a blanket and his apprentices awkwardly standing by.

"I wish you to carefully remove the stones about this place," said the Bishop with a solemn voice and gestured towards the floor beneath the regimental plaque. The men rolled up their sleeves and went to work as the Captain watched with a dry throat. The mason worked carefully with a hammer and chisel. Steadily, he chipped away at the ancient mortar with dull clangs that echoed around the vast interior. The crowd stood watching with wide eyes and the Bishop held his knuckle to his lips.

"This stone has not been removed since the church was remodelled more than three centuries ago," said the mason, as with effort, he heaved it aside with the help of his apprentices.

The gathered party peered into an exposed hole. There, lay a tiny skeleton next to a small wooden box. The mason carefully removed the box and passed it up, into the shaking hands of the Bishop. He opened it and removed a small piece of parchment paper. Then he read with a quavering voice, " 'Dearest one, may God bless you, whom so ever you may be. Here is the body of my poor child who died upon his birth in the year of our Lord 1068. Please look kindly upon his gentle soul. Afford him a proper burial for surely our Lord hath led you to this secret place and allowed his soul and mine to rest in peace.' "

The Bishop declared that he had indeed been guided to this place by the hand of God. The retinue knelt in awed prayer as the cathedral cat licked his paws.

The Bishop's reputation as a very holy man spread and even the King was moved to visit him. Several weeks later, the child was given a Christian burial within the cathedral in a corner of the Lady Chapel. The Captain sat at the rear of the company as the word *Amen* echoed around him.

The next year, at the conclusion of Midnight Mass, at the appointed hour, as the silver disk of the clock aligned with the angel above, the Captain waited and watched. To his satisfaction, the lady in black did not appear. There was only a mouse with twitching whiskers which the Captain allowed to scuttle away.

THE SECRET CAVE

It was the year 1588 and little Brigid's universe was a small island called Oilean Dairbhre: a ragged, windswept scrap of land of a few miles, which clung to the rocky, winding coast of south-west Ireland. She lived there in a tumbledown cottage with her mam and dad, her brothers, and a gentle giant of a black and white cat called the Captain, her constant companion.

The family was poor and life was hard. They survived by growing vegetables and by labouring when work could be found. When she wasn't helping her mam with chores, or mending, or baking, Brigid would wander the craggy coast with the Captain where she explored the salty caves and inhabited a world of magic and make-believe. This world was filled with legends of Annwn, the Otherworld, of faeries, giants, elves and especially of the magician, Mug Ruith, who was said to have lived on Oilean Dairbhre in the ancient past. For Brigid, the legend was as alive as she was, and as real as the conversations that she had with her cat. Her brothers would gently tease her and her parents would smile when she would tell them about her talking cat, and she would entertain them around the evening fire with her imaginings and adventures.

It was a misty and timeless place, where one day melted into the next and the seasons turned as though the world were balanced upon a great wheel.

It was early one morning as Brigid lay in her cot, that she heard her father talking very quietly in serious tones to her mother. He was saying that a fleet of ships was come from far away in a place called *Spanish*. A great sea battle had been fought and the invaders had been forced to sail around the whole of England and Scotland to be able to return home. Now they may be coming to Ireland. She heard her mother gasp and ask in a trembling voice what they should do. She had never heard her father sound more grave as she lay there, pretending to be asleep. He said that they must pray and that they must keep a sharp eye for the invaders who may land upon the coast to murder them in their beds.

That day, as the white gulls wheeled high above in the cobalt blue sky, Brigid made her way with the Captain to her secret cave which lay nestled in the cliff-side, hidden from prying eyes between two great crags.

"We must make a spell like Mug Ruith," she said and the Captain made a little sound.

From a secret hiding place she pulled a small tinderbox and a candle. With practiced fingers she lit the candle in the half-light and her shadow danced upon the slate wall. Solemnly and with great care she next took a stick and scratched a circle in the pebbles and seaweed that lay strewn upon the cave floor. The Captain watched her with dark eyes as Brigid stood in the circle and turned around three times. She closed her eyes and raised her arms.

"I call upon the great wizard, Mug Ruith. Make the winds blow and blow and blow the Spanish away. Protect my mam and dad and my brothers, Kendal and Fergus. Protect the people of your Oilean Dairbhre and blow their ships away."

With that she took a deep breath, looked at the Captain and with great drama and with all her might, she blew the candle out. Smiling and satisfied with her work she cuddled her cat.

"There, that should do it," she said.

When they returned back to the little cottage the air smelled sweetly of home. Her mother was baking, but wearing a worried expression.

"Everything will be alright, Mam," she said.

Her mother smiled. "Well bless your heart."

Morning became afternoon and as the Captain slept, curled into a circle on Brigid's bed, mother and child baked and looked out of the window towards the sea's horizon. There, the sky was slowly turning to the threatening colour of lead. The brightness of the green hillside, lit by the golden afternoon sun, made the island feel all the more vulnerable as the sky became a menacing inky black. The first breeze began to ruffle the leaves of the sparse trees about the house. The warmth of the afternoon was replaced by an unseasonal chill and the sun seemed to drown in darkness as it slid below the horizon. Night was sudden and ominous. Brigid's father and brothers returned from their labour in the field blowing into their cupped hands as they entered the little cottage.

"There's a nasty storm brewing. We shouldn't be doing it so soon but we're putting up the shutters," said her father as he and the boys busied themselves to cover the windows against the impending weather.

That night, the wind howled as it had never howled within living memory. The rain beat down with the sound of a thousand giants' drumming and the surf breaking upon the cliff was like the devil slamming the great doors in the halls of hell. The little family sat huddled together with their animals and waited for the darkness to pass. It blew all night, all day, and all night again. Finally, on the second morning, the sun glimmered in the sky and the family made their way outside, blinking in the still, bright air. Trees were uprooted, pieces of wood and fence lay all about and the chicken coop had disappeared.

"Well, it's lucky the birds took shelter with us," said Brigid's dad as he comforted her mam.

"Look Dad!" shouted Kendall, pointing.

There in the distance, they saw soldiers from the mainland heading for the coast nearby.

"Everyone stay here," said Brigid's dad and he set off to investigate. When he returned he looked sad and shook his head. "The men from Spanish are no more," he said.

Brigid gasped.

"Their ships are wrecked all up and down the coast.* One called the *Trinidad* is wrecked upon our very island shore and those unlucky enough to survive have been rounded up by the soldiers and are to be

---

* Due to severe storms, between 17 and 24 ships of the Spanish Armada of 1588 were lost on the Irish coast including the *Trinidad*. This accounted for about one-third of the fleet's total loss of 63 ships and of about 5,000 men.

hanged, poor devils."

Brigid pressed her knuckle to her mouth and burst into tears.

Over the next few days, the little family busied themselves by mending their fences and repairing their damaged roof. The chicken coop was repaired with the debris that still lay all about. With the help of neighbours, valuable stores were dragged from the beach where the evidence of the wrecked *Trinidad* lay strewn upon the rocks. A tangle of broken rigging, ripped sail, mangled wood, rope and iron lay scattered for miles upon the rocky coast. People were hailing the storm as a miracle and thanked the good Lord for their deliverance from the murderous Spanish. Brigid remained subdued, but she had her old Captain to cuddle and as long as that was the case, her small world would always be filled with light and with hope.

In a few days, life on Oilean Dairbhre returned to relative normality and Brigid took the opportunity to slip away with the Captain. She wanted to return to her secret cave where she would quietly say a prayer. The brightness of the day and the warmth of the sun lifted her spirits and she giggled as she ran along with the Captain trotting after her as dutifully as the finest breed of gun dog. Carefully, she lowered herself down the cliff face where she knew all the foot and hand holds to round the crag and as she did, she gasped. There, impossibly, halfway down the cliff and wedged in the mouth of her cave was a small boat. She swallowed as she tried to imagine the force of a wave that could have lifted the little vessel to such a height, for the sea surged upon the rocks far, far below. The Captain followed her as she arrived at the mouth of the cave. The little boat was wedged half on its side. A pool of sea water filled it to the gunnel where a single smashed oar hung forlornly. Brigid squeezed past the boat which, scratched and battered as it was, clearly bore the name of the *Trinidad*. She moved further into the cave and stopped suddenly as the Captain hissed a warning. There, lying propped up against the slate cave wall, was a man clutching a sword. Upon seeing Brigid he laid the sword aside and weakly raised an arm. Brigid backed away with a fearful face.

"Child, I will not hurt you," he said with a thick accent.

Brigid, her eyes adjusting to the half-light of the cave, noticed how pale he was, and how ragged. His clothes were dark red and blue; embroidered with gold thread and torn at the shoulder. His leg was twisted, his face bruised, and one eye was blackened and swollen shut.

Brigid picked up the Captain and held him against her as though for protection. She asked in a small voice, "Who are you and why did you come here?"

"I am Rodrigo de Cuéllar Cervantes, officer aboard his Majesty Phillip II's ship, *Trinidad* of 800 tons, lost these days past upon this coast. My arrival here is quite accidental I assure you. We are sorry that we embarked upon this sorry adventure. We were sailing for home," he paused, "for Spain."

The man gingerly touched his head. His one eye blinked. "That is a most wonderful and prodigious cat."

"He's the Captain and he's magical," said Brigid with pride.

The man smiled. It was genuine and kind.

"Ah, magical, is he? Can he cast a spell to take me home?"

Brigid looked at the man guiltily and then burst into tears. The man looked distressed.

"It's my fault," she said between sobs.

"Dear child. What is your fault?"

"I said a spell to make the wind blow."

The man smiled again. "I have a daughter of about your age and she believes in magic too. Please do not be distressed. The storm was being made many days ago far out at sea. You did not cause the winds to blow."

Brigid looked at him uncertainly.

"Let me show you a magic trick," said the man. "Come closer."

Brigid stood still, but the Captain, sensing the man's good heart, jumped down, trotted across the cave and sniffed at the man's clothes. The man showed Brigid his empty hands and then reached behind the Captain's ear. With a flourish he produced a coin. Brigid clapped her hands with excitement. The man held the coin in the air, waved his other hand over it, and then opened his hands wide to show that it had disappeared. Brigid beamed and clapped again. The man smiled and after a pause said, "I have a question for you. Where am I?"

Brigid and the man sat together. She told him all about the island and the soldiers as he listened with a sad frown. He told her about his home and the orange trees that grew in his garden; about his children, his wife, his dogs and his horses. As they spoke, the Captain sat quietly, listening. The afternoon was growing late and Brigid told the man that she had to go. She invited him to her cottage so that he could eat something and meet her mam and dad, and Kendall and Fergus. The man smiled.

"You are very gracious, but I fear that if I were to accept your invitation I may place your family in danger. However, I am very hungry and the water that I have been collecting from the rocks has dried away in the sun."

"You cannot live here," said Brigid.

"I have a slim chance. I know there are other ships sailing home and passing this shore. Each evening I make my way down to the beach below and signal in the hope that they may see and send a boat to pick me up. Fortunately, this place is well hidden. A hot and smokeless signal fire in the evening can only be seen from the sea. In the meantime, can I ask for your discretion and keep my presence here a secret of ours?"

The man offered his hand.

"I will keep your secret and promise to bring you some bread and some water," said Brigid. She reached forward and shook the Spaniard's hand with great formality. He thanked her with a bow of his head and watched her leave, followed by the Captain, who looked back over his shoulder and blinked.

The next morning, Brigid and the Captain returned with half a loaf of bread, two boiled eggs, a flask of water and a blanket from her bed. The man thanked her, bit into the bread and closed his eyes.

"Never has bread tasted so good as this," he said smiling at her with watery eyes.

"I baked it. Mam helped," said Brigid.

"You are an angel," said the man. "Thank you for your help and for your trust."

Brigid was surprised to see a tear quietly roll down the man's cheek as he ate. She and the Captain sat watching him. When he had finished eating, he leaned back and smiled at the seriousness of Brigid's expression.

"This magician that you mentioned when we first met..."

Brigid beamed and said, "Mug Ruith. His breath could cause storms or turn men to stone."

"Yes, Mug Ruith. If you could meet this Mug Ruith what magic would you ask him to perform?"

She stood in her frayed, darned smock and a little crease appeared on her forehead as she concentrated and then the words came tumbling out. "I would ask him to caste a spell so that my dad would not work himself to death in the fields and so that Kendall and Fergus could learn to read and we would be free to go to school and Mam wouldn't cry any more and we could eat every day."

The man looked at Brigid. "That is a lot of magic to perform."

"I know," she said quietly. "I'd best be getting back. I'll bring you more food tomorrow."

"The soldiers are back!" shouted Fergus, peering through the little window as the early morning sun filtered into the ramshackle cottage. Brigid's mam and dad exchanged worried glances. Brigid rushed to the door and opened it, allowing the Captain to slip out.

"And where do you think you're going young lady?" said her mam, pulling her back.

Brigid ran to the window and looked out with Fergus and Kendall. The men from the mainland carried crossbows and pikes and were marching in the direction of Brigid's secret cave. As the family watched, sprinting past the soldiers, was the familiar black and white shape of the Captain running at full-tilt.

The Captain's heart pounded in his chest as he reached the cliff-top and saw that there, anchored in the bay, was a ship. Closer, being rowed towards the shore, was a boat. Hurriedly, the Captain made his way down the cliff-side to the cave. The man was sleeping, curled up under his blanket. The Captain barked at him, "Rodrigo, wake up."

The man's eye opened and widened as he recognized the Captain.

"I am dreaming," he said uncertainly.

"This is no dream," said the Captain. "Your boat is here but there are soldiers on their way, alerted by the ship in the bay. You must move as quickly as you can."

"This is the strangest dream I have ever had," said the man blinking.

The Captain lunged forward and bit the man's hand. He recoiled and put his hand to his mouth in shock.

"This is real and you speak Spanish. You're a…cat."

"Time is short," hissed the Captain.

The man scrambled to his feet.

"Grab the blanket and the water flask. Brigid cannot be implicated in your protection. It would be very bad for all the people of Oilean Dairbhre. Quickly now."

The man followed his instructions and hurried out of the cave. Upon seeing him emerge from the cave, the sailors in the boat cheered, looking up as they neared the beach and shipped their oars.

"Follow me," said the Captain, "I know the quickest way down."

The man scrambled after the cat as quickly as his injured leg would carry him. They found the beach near the man's still smouldering signal fire from the evening before.

"Get into the boat and tell the oarsmen to break their backs," commanded the Captain.

Above, they could hear shouted orders. An officer in the boat was standing and saluted as they neared. The man splashed through the shallow water and fell into the arms of the sailors.

"I am relieved to see you alive, Admiral," said the officer.

A bolt from a crossbow above, hit the water as the oarsmen strained to push off from the beach. The boat grated upon the pebbles and then, as the water deepened, it glided smoothly away. The man was looking back at the black and white cat on the shoreline and called out, "Tell Brigid I have buried the spell of Mug Ruith in the corner of her cave, under the white stone. And thank you, Captain. You are indeed a most magical cat." He finished with a salute.

The Captain could hear the officer asking the man if he was alright. His laugh of relief by way of reply echoed across the water. The Captain looked up and saw the soldiers clambering down the cliff-side; swarming around the broken boat at the cave. Quietly, he hid himself from sight as the soldiers searched the cave and beach. Out in the bay, the ship's sails gleamed in the morning sun and then, gently listing under the pressure of the breeze, she glided away majestically for Spain. The soldiers on the beach could only look on and remarked to themselves, that no guns were fired at them from on board. The Captain remained concealed until dark and then made his way along the beach, and back to Brigid and home.

"They say that he'd been living in the cave since the storm and the shipwreck," said Brigid's dad to her mam.

"Well who would have thought of such a thing."

They were on their way, with Brigid, Fergus and Kendall as the Captain trotted behind them, to see the cave where the drama had taken place. The once secret cave had become infamous and highly visited by the island residents. It had been several weeks since the Spanish ship had sailed out of the bay and the boat from the *Trinidad* had long since disappeared, having been claimed as salvage. Indeed, this was the case with most of the remnants of the *Trinidad* itself, so that little remained that would suggest that anything unusual had happened on Oilean Dairbhre at all.

Brigid, the boys and her dad climbed down and stood in Brigid's cave while her mam enjoyed the warm sunshine above. Brigid saw that in the corner, amongst broken slate and lying undisturbed, was a white stone from the beach below, just as the Captain had described to her.

"Dad, can I talk with you?" said Brigid.

The boys shrugged and left to keep their mam company. When they had gone, Brigid told her father the whole story.

"Come now, Brigid," he said when she had finished, "you know we like your stories but we should be getting back."

The Captain was scratching at the slate by the white stone.

"Please Dad. Please move those big stones where the Captain says."

Brigid's dad pursed his lips together and he gave her a long look, as if to say that enough is enough, but the expression on her face and the love that he felt for his daughter made him roll up his sleeves and start to dig with his hands at the heavy pile of slate. After working for ten minutes he stopped suddenly and looked around at Brigid with a shocked expression. She was watching anxiously, her hands clenched. With effort he pulled out a heavy metal box. It was unlocked and he sat down, shocked, when he opened the lid to reveal the golden coins within the strongbox of His Majesty Phillip II's ship *Trinidad.*

Many years later, Brigid travelled to Valencia in Spain with her husband, an eminent physician from Dublin, and colleague of her brother Fergus. They had lunch with a retired Admiral in his garden, and as he asked after her magical cat, long since departed from this world and laid to rest in a special cave, the sweet and fragrant smell of orange blossoms was carried to them upon the gentle breeze.

THE LETTERS FROM "THE BLESSING"

12 March 1723

My dearest George,

How I am looking forward to coming home to you and to dear sweet England. It is wonderful to see Meg fully recovered, though I must confess, that throughout my time here, I have missed everything about dear Hadley Hall. How wonderful it will be to see the rose garden again. Is Binky still missing me awfully?

Since setting sail from Boston, the voyage has been quite tedious, with unrelenting stormy weather for the past week! Many of the passengers aboard have suffered from sea sickness which has hindered social interaction and has prevented me from making the acquaintance of Lady Stepney. I had hoped her Ladyship would invite us up to London during the season. Apparently, Lady Stepney detests the sea and has a marked aversion to the motion of any ship, so this weather must be quite a trial for her. Captain Figg has assured us that *The Blessing* is sound and that the weather will not impede progress. He says that there is much time left to, in his words, "enjoy" the voyage, which I thought a little impertinent. How I long for this to end.

15 March 1723

Dearest George,

Fortunately, the weather has improved over the last two days and the spirits of all aboard have lifted considerably. Today, I took a turn up on deck. How marvellous to look up at the billowing sails as the ship rushes through the water and the moon high in the blue sky. The moon is so beautiful at sea. The colour and smell of the ocean was quite sublime. It was very fine indeed.

17 March 1723

Darling George,

Since I began writing these letters something most curious has occurred. Last evening I was invited to dine with the captain and his first officers. You can imagine my excitement upon hearing that Lady Stepney was gracious enough to also accept an invitation affording me an excellent opportunity to make a good impression upon her.

Well, in truth, the evening was rather dull and conversation somewhat strained until Mr Evans, the first officer, told us a most amusing story concerning a member of the crew. Apparently, the crewman had been a master on various slavers but had finished up his service as gunner aboard HMS *Swallow*. You may recall, darling, that this was the ship which successfully fought and defeated the pirate, *Royal Fortune,* in that most famous and bloody battle off the coast of West Africa last year.[*] The fellow claims that after the engagement he took off the ship's cat and cared for it. This cat was said to be the companion of the defeated pirate, Captain Bartholomew Roberts (Black Bart), who had been killed in the violence of the exchange. Mr Evans fears that after years of service, the poor old seaman is suffering from some mental challenge, for he claims that this cat is able to communicate in both English and Spanish! You can imagine how we were amused by this assertion and Mr Evans told the story with marked gusto. It seems that the creature (the cat) is quite ancient—upward of thirty and five years and is travelling home to England to live in retirement with this amusing crew member who is on his final voyage. We could not resist but to implore Mr Evans to introduce us to this fellow which he promised to do at dinner the

---

[*] This sea battle was fought on February 10th, 1722, at Cape Lopez Bay, Gabon.

following evening. As good as his word, this evening, we were joined by the seaman who seemed rather ill at ease but very polite. Presumably, he was on his best behaviour (I feel sure that the presence of Lady Stepney encouraged his good demeanour). His table manners clearly indicated that he was of a low station, not used to polite society, and he introduced himself as Charley Johnson. Mr. Evans asked him to re-tell the story of the cat which seemed to make him nervous so that he quite stammered. Those around the table smiled, for we felt sure that the fellow knew that his tale would be shown to be a foolish concoction and that the game was up. Seemingly undaunted and with a straight face, he told us of having found the cat on the pirate gun deck. He was told that the animal was a very close companion of Roberts and should therefore be thrown overboard in a weighted sack to join his infamous friend in Davy Jones's locker. Feeling pity for it, the fellow smuggled the cat aboard the *Swallow* and the crew fed him from the rations of their own plates. That seemed to be the end of it, until Mr Evans prompted him to continue his story. Awkwardly, this Mr Johnson told us that after a few days the cat seemed to be saying "thanks" to the crew for his food, which amused them greatly, for you hear of animals that have developed a way of imitating human sound. However, it seems that the extent of the animal's powers did not end there, for one evening, when Johnson fed the cat it suggested an improvement to the performance of the ship.

"And what was this suggestion?" asked Mr Evans.

"Well, the cat told me the ship was ardent, sir, that she carried too much weather helm."

"And what did you reply, Mr Johnson?" asked Captain Figg.

"Well, I was so stunned, sir, that all I could think was to ask it what was to be done."

How we all laughed at this and the captain raised a glass.

"And what did the cat suggest?" asked the captain.

"Well, he said it was on account of the added weight of goods and crew seized from his ship *The Fortune*. He said that it had created instability and the ship should be re-organized to find her best centre of lateral resistance. Failing that, we could try shortening sail with close attention on reefing top-sails and topgallants."

You may imagine, dear George, how the officers roared with laughter at this absurdity.

"What did you think to this suggestion?" asked our captain.

"I thought he made a very good point, sir," replied the fellow.

They roared again.

"You have had other conversations with this most remarkable animal I understand," said Mr Evans.

"Indeed, sir, he has related to me some wonderful stories concerning the history of the robberies and murders of the most notorious pirates."[*]

At this, Lady Stepney said that she had heard enough nonsense and that clearly the entertainment was better suited to the pages of some popular novel by Mr Defoe. Mr Johnson went quite red in the face and the table was quiet. Undeterred, Mr Evans suggested that there was a simple way in which the story could be proved or disproved.

"And what is that, Mr Evans?" asked Lady Stepney with clear impatience.

"Obviously, this cat must be interviewed."

Lady Stepney looked so scornful, George, that I felt most embarrassed for Mr Johnson who I thought had played his role in the joke with great perfection, for as you know, seamen love their stories.

"I am afraid, sir, that simply won't do," said Mr Johnson quietly.

"Oh? Why so?" replied Mr Evans.

"The cat is very ancient and has been suffering these last few weeks. He is off his food as there was only biscuit to eat and mutters only in Spanish on occasion," replied Mr Johnson with such unabashed sincerity that the humour around the table was quite restored.

"Bravo," said Mr Evans, "you are a most amusing storyteller, Mr Johnson."

---

[*] The original authoritative record of the golden age of piracy, *A General History of the Robberies and murders of the most notorious Pyrates,* was published in London in 1724 with great success. The identity of its author, one Captain Charles Johnson, remains a mystery to this day.

Seeming to see a gracious way out of his obvious predicament the fellow thanked his host and the conversation turned to other things. I thought that this must be the end of the matter, but Lady Stepney was quite vehement in pursuit of poor Mr Johnson. I felt sure that the recent bad weather must be the reason for her poor temper, for she asked, "So you claim the cat will speak Spanish, Mr Johnson? I am most familiar with that, ahem, lengua. Bring it to us."

"I'm afraid he won't come," replied Mr Johnson looking flustered.

At this, the most amusing Mr Evans carved a succulent piece of meat from the delicious bird that we had been enjoying and with a wink to the table, instructed Mr Johnson to take this to the cat and to inform him that he would be well rewarded for a brief visit. Presumably seeing no way out of his predicament, Mr Johnson carefully took the meat in his fingers, rose to his feet and said he would see what could be done. Upon leaving, Mr Evans said that there was clearly no hope for the fellow and let that be the end of it. Lady Stepney snorted and we all assumed that we would not see Mr Johnson again that evening, for surely he would not attempt to continue his charade. Conversation turned to matters of the ship, but imagine our surprise when not twenty minutes later there was a knock upon the door. Captain Figg raised a quizzical eyebrow as he said, "Come in."

Mr Johnson returned carrying a great bundle which he set down at his own place setting. There, swathed in a ship's blanket, was an enormous black and white cat, so prodigious that I have never seen its like. He was easily twice the size of dear Binky. We were all quite taken aback as the beast stared around at us with, I must say George, one large yellow eye.

"Don't you mind his looks, ladies. It's on account of an incident with grapeshot in a battle off the Whydah Coast some years back," said Mr Johnson without a trace of irony. I glanced at Lady Stepney who seemed quite put off her food and was looking at the creature with undisguised disgust. I must confess that anyone would have much reason to sympathize with her. It seemed to me that the animal had suffered an extreme trauma at some time which had resulted in the considerable loss of fur and an eye.

"What is that on its head?" Captain Figg asked uncertainly.

"'Tis a pig's ear, sir," replied Mr Johnson.

"A pig's ear, man?"

"Yes sir, for his own was ripped off his head by grapeshot you see. He gave instructions for this one to replace it so that he may continue his mouse and ratting duties. For to listen with, you understand. I think the sailmaker made a handsome job of it. True 'tis a little bit on the large side, but the Captain (is his name), says it serves admirably well, something like a hearing trumpet but permanently affixed."

At this Lady Stepney looked quite ill.

"And what is that?" asked Captain Figg, pointing.

"Is his leg, sir. A result of an altercation with an ornery baboon some years ago. The leg was too bad to be saved but the baboon came of worse: stone dead he was. The ship's carpenter carved this leg from hardest mahogany and the Captain gets around on it tolerably well."

"Really!" muttered Lady Stepney. "Can we get on!"

I must confess, George, that I glanced at Mr Evans at this point and could see that he regarded her Ladyship with patient bitterness. "Come, your Ladyship," he said evenly, "do you not think this a most remarkable creature?"

"I do not!" was the curt reply. "I find both this creature and Mr Johnson quite ridiculous and I am tired of this charade."

"Yes, enough of this, I think Mr Evans. Take the animal away please, Mr Johnson," said Captain Figg.

Dear George, while this conversation had been taking place I had been watching the creature closely. The entire time, he had been examining the roast bird with that one large yellow eye. He now turned to look at me, and I must say my darling, that never have I been looked at in such a way by any animal. There seemed to be such depth, I may say, an intelligence! I felt that I must intercede on the poor creature's behalf, so in spite of possible injury to my relationship with Lady Stepney, I turned to Captain Figg and pleaded the cat's case. "Dear Captain Figg, will it be said that we have reneged on a promise? Regardless of whether it was made to man or beast a promise was made to reward the animal's presence. It will take but a moment to carve some meat for the poor creature."

"How can you resist such a heartfelt plea, sir?" remarked Mr Evans with a mischievous wink.

"Very well," said Captain Figg and her Ladyship huffed.

Mr Evans dutifully carved what can only be described as a small, succulent feast and laid it before the animal. Slowly, it looked around at the gathered company and then stretched, arching it's great back in such a fashion that we could feel the entire table shake. However, just as the animal dipped its head to eat, Lady Stepney reached out and snatched away the plate. The cat looked at her for a moment and then made the most extraordinary sound. It was like the shout of a child, something like a whine, but spat out with a forceful passion at the interruption. Unmistakably, this vehemence was directed toward Lady Stepney who was visibly taken aback by the violence of it. For a moment she stared at the creature as the blood seemed to drain from her face. She seemed unable to speak and then, unsteadily, she rose to her feet. She was gripping the table so hard that her knuckles showed white and she gasped in a choked voice, "I have never been, never, never been so insulted."

To our astonishment she simply left the room. The cat was casually eating from the plate. We all looked at each other in some shock. Captain Figg admonished Mr Johnson who sheepishly apologized, gathered up the animal, and left.

"We will hear no more of cats please, Mr Evans," said Captain Figg.

Mr Evans was obviously embarrassed and the evening remained subdued for the rest of the courses. Lady Stepney did not return.

Throughout the rest of dinner I could not help but keep thinking about the episode and wondering what could have affected Lady Stepney in this way. There was, I confess, something very strange and disquieting about the encounter and yet I am fascinated by what could have caused such a reaction from her Ladyship. Darling George, the hour grows late. How I long to be home. Good-night and sweet dreams.

26 March 1723

My darling George,

I have the worst of news, for the terrible weather has caught up with us again. We thought that it was a bad storm when we left Boston, but indeed, that was the merest squall in comparison to the gale with which we are now confronted. At this very moment, the ship is tossed about as though it were but a tiny fragment of flotsam upon the churning sea. The creaking and groaning of the boards about my cabin is, I must confess, of great concern to me. I wish that you were here, my darling, to give me strength and hold me tight.

27 March 1723

My darling,

It is as though the ocean conspires to ruin us. I could not have imagined, in my worst nightmares, the size of the swell that the ship is riding upon. At one moment we are in the deepest trough and the next we are cresting a mountain staring into the abyss. I have not seen Captain Figg who has spent the last eighteen hours upon the bridge, but I was called upon by Lieutenant Evans who was kindly enquiring after my well being. Although he did his best to reassure me as to our safety and to disguise his concern, I could not help but see the strain and worry upon his face. I cannot begin to describe to you the terrible screaming noise of the wind. We all remain in our cabins and social entertainment is quite out of the question. Lady Stepney is apparently very ill from the extreme motion of the ship and has been visited upon by the ship's surgeon, Mr Cross (quite a grumpy and tall fellow—in all completely unsuited to his profession).

28 March 1723

My dearest darling,

Will you ever read these letters? The storm continues in its ferocity and I have grave news. Today, I was trying to sleep when I heard the most awful crack and much shouting from the crew on deck. That was followed by the most thunderous boom and the ship shuddered and went over. My darling, I have never been so frightened. Please excuse the tears that stain the page. Apparently, something called the mizzen-mast was broken under duress which caused the ship to "yaw" (which means to lose its course). This resulted in our being hit broadside by a wave which has apparently opened the ship's seams. My dearest darling, Captain Figg came to see me. I must say he was a tower of strength, but told me that he must give me bad news so that I should not hear rumours from some other source. The ship is taking on water. The sailors who are not on deck are taking turns at the pumps. Captain Figg says that they are keeping the water level at bay and have jury-rigged another mizzen. That means that the mast has been repaired. Above the howling wind I heard the most terrible screaming today. Apparently, Lady Stepney is quite hysterical. Dr Cross was not in good spirits.

30 March 1723

Darling George,

Yesterday, I slept for the whole day. At last, the massive seas have subsided and have returned to something closer to normality. However, upon waking I realized that my cabin was leaning at an unmistakable angle. I immediately went in search of Captain Figg who, I was told, was looking at the bilge. I asked that when he was finished looking at the bilge would he be kind enough to call upon me. Some hours later, Captain Figg called and I asked him how long it took to look at the bilge? Immediately I regretted treating him harshly, however. The poor fellow seemed quite exhausted. He explained that the ship was listing, (which is the nautical term for lean) because of the water which was coming in faster than his crew was able to pump it out. He said that time was against us and should the situation continue it would create something of a problem.

"Now, if you will excuse me, madam, I have urgent matters to attend to."

And then he abruptly left, leaving me feeling quite put out. Within moments I determined to go after him and tell him he should improve his manners. I left my cabin and who should I immediately bump into but Mr Johnson.

"Did you see Captain Figg, Mr Johnson?"

"I was going to ask you the same thing, miss."

"Indeed?"

"I've got a message for him, 'scuse me miss."

With that he was off.

I returned to my cabin and fumed. I must confess, and you know this to be true my darling, that I fume when I am worried. I fumed greatly, and for hours.

Late in the afternoon, I heard more shouts and yells from on deck above my cabin. I couldn't stand the claustrophobia any longer and determined to see what was going on. Putting on my outer coat and gloves and holding the wall as the ship swayed, I made my way up to the main deck where, so recently during clement weather, I had revelled in taking the air. As I made my way out into the lashing rain I saw that the sea was grey and swollen. Oh, but how joyous to breath fresh air! The sailors were very busy and I was careful to keep to one side and you may be sure, hold on very tightly as Mr Evans had shown me. Looking up at the bridge, I was amazed to see Mr Johnson standing next to Captain Figg like an officer. He was braced against the railing and holding a bundle in his arms. I squinted through the rain and realized that the bundle was in fact the enormous cat which had so upset Lady Stepney. Watching, it seemed that, (I know this seems absurd), that the cat was communicating with Captain Figg who strained to listen to his meow and then called instructions down to the sailors on deck. They were arranged in what is termed "gangs" and were hauling on ropes with all their might. It was at this moment, my darling, as I watched their straining faces and desperate efforts that I fully realized the peril that we were in.

"Madam, you must come below."

It was Lieutenant Evans shouting in the driving rain and urging me below decks. I acquiesced, but insisted that he tell me what was happening. When we had descended the ladder to relative quiet out of the storm, he told me that they were using an innovative method to staunch the leak. A sail was being hauled beneath the ship and in theory, the relative pressure of the ocean should hold it close for long enough to pump out the bilge and allow the carpenter to make repairs.

"Where did this innovation hail from, Mr Evans?" I asked.

For the first time I saw him blush. He must have seen the surprise on my face for he excused himself and stumbled away.

My darling the hour is late and the sea is calmer. Good night my darling. Sweet dreams.

31 March 1723

My dearest darling, George,

Three things have happened today which I thought I should never see. The first is that the ship has stopped its dreadful listing. The poor crew I am told have never ceased their pumping and the innovative and well placed sail has given them a chance to catch up. The carpenters have executed their repairs and we are sailing once more for England and home to you my darling.

The second is that the sun is shining. Oh Joy! I was up on deck today and what a pleasure to see the ship coursing through the water with ease once more. Looking up, I saw Captain Figg. He waved to me and I have quite forgiven him.

The third is this: I decided to go below decks (as it is called) and pay a visit to Mr Johnson. My curiosity, as you know my darling, does not allow me to rest. After much meandering down in that dark and furtive wooden world, I came upon what I was assured was Mr Johnson's cabin on what is termed as the orlop. The door seemed very tiny and as I stooped to knock, I thought I heard voices. Please forgive me, but I could not help myself—I peered through the key-hole. There were but two inhabitants of the cabin. The first was the old cat which was blinking its great yellow eye and wearing its pig's ear. To my shock and in plain view, the second occupant was Lady Stepney. She seemed to be sobbing and spoke to the cat with much fondness, as though he were a favourite child! It was then that I noticed that she was hand feeding him white flesh which she pulled with her fingers from a roasted chicken! I took great care to tip-toe away and save any embarrassment on either side. I fear that the storm may have induced a brain fever in her Ladyship and will mention something to grumpy Dr Cross.

I love you darling and long to be home again.

Your loving wife,

Margarette

THE SEANCE

The Captain belonged to the cook, Mrs Potts, who it must be said, worshipped the big old cat and celebrated the fact that he ensured that her kitchen, pantry, scullery and stores were free of any mouse or rat. For these duties he was rewarded generously with a warm place to sleep by the stove and many tasty morsels which he ate from a small blue and white saucer by the back door.

The kitchen was located in the basement of a large tall house, in a large tall square, adorned with white façade and ornate wrought iron railings. The difference between this house and all the others in their neat, numbered rows was that at this house the curtains remained drawn. This was a sign that the house was in a state of deep mourning, for the master of the house, Sir Lionel Grasper, had died six months previously in the year of our Lord, 1860. His widow, Lady Grasper, dressed in black silk crepe, remained largely indoors and would observe the state of deep mourning for a year. The rooms upstairs were dark and swathed in black, the clocks were stopped at the hour of Sir Lionel's death (ten minutes to two) and the servants (who also wore black), were careful to maintain a respectful hush at all times. The Captain, who mainly occupied the rooms below stairs, occasionally made silent and stealthy excursions up among the dark shrouded and heavily swathed twilight of Lady Grasper's world. He would take care that he would not be seen, as he disappeared behind a heavy curtain to stare out of a window into the bright square below. Unobserved, he would curl up in the magnified watery sunlight and watch the carriages, cabs and buggies, their horses' hooves echoing, as they came and went. The tradespeople, pushing their ubiquitous barrows and venturing with obeisant gratitude into the realm of society tended to the multifarious needs of the square's inhabitants: at one end the coalman delivers and at the other the sweep removes; at one end the midwife delivers and at the other the undertaker removes. And so on. But nobody bothered the house with the curtains drawn. The house in mourning lay undisturbed, the hands of its clocks silently raised in ironic surrender to the inevitability of mortality at ten to two. As afternoon drew on, the Captain would return silently to the kitchen where Mrs Potts would be preparing dinner with the help of little Lottie, the scullery maid. The two would coo over him and pop some giblets into his saucer and he would blink at them in gratitude and tuck in.

This stately hibernation was interrupted one day by a visit from Lady Grasper's friend and confidante, Mrs Caroline Gush, who arrived in a state of flushed and breathless excitement. She was ushered into the morning room (which felt more like evening in the lightless murk) for an audience with her Ladyship. This is part of the conversation that Agnes the housemaid heard, as instead of polishing the grate in the side room, she stood with her ear pressed against the door of the morning room across the hall:

"Dear Caroline, whatever is the matter?"

"I'm so sorry Georgina, but I am quite beside myself and felt bound to come and see you, my dearest friend, with some quite extraordinary news."

"Indeed? What news could inspire such excitement?"

"Please, don't be too shocked when I tell you that…that I have spoken to daddy."

"But surely…"

"Wait, I know what you are going to say but let me explain. There is an extraordinary man in town just lately travelled up from the country at the invitation of the Countess Froud. Georgina, this man is what they call a medium. His name is Dr Connor and he is, apparently, a member of the most high order of Druids or something. Anyway," (speaking breathlessly) "this fellow is well known in society. The Countess was quite overwhelmed when, at her house in town, this doctor communicated with Count Froud. Well, just last night I accompanied Anne Temple to an evening at the Countess's where we all sat around a table with the doctor who asked if there was anybody there. Shortly thereafter, the doctor slipped into what they call a trance and the Count signalled his presence with a knock and spoke through him. The Countess said that it was unmistakably him. Well, later he asked if there was anyone called Caroline in the room, for there was a gentleman with a message for her. I told him that my name was Caroline and sure enough, he spoke in daddy's voice to tell me that he was happy on the other side and I shouldn't be sorry at his passing. He said that he and mummy were together again. Isn't it wonderful?"

At this point, Mr Haytor, the head butler, could be heard on the stairs below and Agnes was forced to scurry back to the side room grate. Inevitably, rumour of the conversation circulated below stairs and the Captain tilted his head at the breathless whisper of *Druid* on Mrs Potts' lips. Ben Slink, the footman, was dispatched with a note from Lady Grasper to Countess Froud.

The next day, word came from Mr Haytor that a dinner for ten was to be organized for the following week which would include Countess Froud and her house guest.

"Ah, it will be like the old days when Sir Lionel was still here," sighed Mrs Potts as she came down from her meeting with Lady Grasper after organizing the menu. This would, it turned out, include cream of mushroom soup, lettuce salad, baked salmon with sauce hollandaise, roast chicken with potato balls, ham timbales with cucumber sauce and green peas, mousse au chocolate, delicate little cakes, lemon sherbet, vanilla ice cream and Brazilian coffee. Mr Haytor self-importantly unlocked the door to the wine cellar to check his inventory.

There was much activity as the dining room was prepared. This involved polishing the table and furniture, and all of the silver candlesticks, knives, forks, spoons, smaller spoons, smaller knives, even smaller spoons and on and on. This left Agnes with black fingers and the lingering, blunt aroma of metal polish for the next several days.

Though the house retained its funereal air, there was a shared sense of expectation amongst the staff. Throughout the preparations, planning and obsessive minutia, the Captain languidly continued in his daily routine and idly watched the people of the square come and go. As he watched, his eyelids would begin to droop, his face settled in his paws, and he would drift off into a comfortable sleep. In his timeless dreamscape, images of cathedrals and castles, of caves and cottages would unwind before him and he would mutter under his breath; his slack jaw lolling and his tongue forming the sound of "leaf" ; an old man's face close to his, smiling. Then he would wake up, his head full of half remembered images, and then he would wash.

The night of the dinner arrived and the upper servants waited in the hall under the direction of Mr Haytor who examined each in turn, adjusting a cuff here, a cap there, until he was satisfied.

Unaware of the impending guests or of the planned event, the Captain was sitting amongst the rows of silver cutlery, licking his paws on the dining room table, having been accidentally trapped in the dining room during the afternoon preparations. Fashionably late, the guests began to arrive. Mr Haytor answered the door, Agnes took hats and coats, and the guests were shown up to the drawing room. Below, in the kitchen, Mrs Potts was timing everything to perfection and dreading any possible delay. In the drawing room, the guests were greeted by Lady Grasper and offered a superior sherry by Slink, the footman, who hovered in white gloves. The Captain could hear the now unfamiliar sound of conversation, but it was the sound of approaching footsteps which prompted him to briefly stretch and drop from the table down onto the Axminster carpet. In his fear of discovery, he secreted himself behind the heavy curtains at the balcony window. The door opened and Mr Haytor came in with stiff necked vigilance to light the candles and make final inspection. He flicked away a cat's hair from the table with a scowl then stepped back and surveyed with satisfaction, the heavy expanse of burnished mahogany, the regimented host of crystal ware, and the arrayed arsenal of silver cutlery glowing in the candlelight.

Slink arrived with a vast tureen, Agnes with a mountain of dainty bread rolls, baked by Mrs Potts that afternoon. Shortly, the privileged and rustling guests meandered in, and with Lady Grasper's help, they diligently arrived at their assigned seating arrangements. Throughout this flurry of activity, no opportunity presented itself to the Captain to make a suitable exit, so he stayed where he was behind the curtain. Mr Haytor brushed past him, reverently brandishing a bottle of Chablis as the soup was served with fawning respect. Amid discrete and subtle slurping and as the silver spoons made tinkling contact with fine bone china, Lady Grasper, eyebrows raised in stately benevolence, surveyed the table. There was her friend, Caroline, with her weak chinned, utterly stupid, but comfortingly wealthy husband, Thomas. There was Anne Temple and her friend Mr Bingham, both of whom looked simply too modern. There was Caroline's sister, Fanny, and her cousin, the giggling Freda. There was her friend, the shy Algernon, to make up the number, and lastly Countess Froud and her guest, the mysterious and other-worldly Dr

Connor. The Countess, well known for her general disdain of humanity, was unquestionably obsequious in the doctor's company. At this very moment, he was the suitably diffident object of her uncharacteristic praise. "Dr Connor has a great knowledge of history. Dr Connor has a remarkable mind for philosophy. Dr Connor has a wonderful eye for art; has a great ear for music; has a nose for these things."

Dr Connor sipped his soup carefully, dabbed gently at his rustic beard with his napkin, held up his hand, and spoke with the indulgent modesty of one who is accustomed to such flattery.

"You do me much honour, Countess, but the small gifts that I possess are not of my making. They have been passed down to me by our ancient ancestors. I am but a servant," (indicating a stiff and shifty Slink with a flourish of his hand) "a humble vassal of the traditional knowledge of our magical past. It is my privilege to be able to bring comfort to the bereaved, to bring comfort to those in need of comforting."

With this he inclined his head towards the Countess who clasped her glittering, bejewelled hands, and sighed. Caroline beamed and said, "These gifts, Dr Connor, how ancient do you suppose them to be?"

Dr Connor narrowed his eyes and held his glass stem up for examination as he contemplated. For a moment the candlelight was defused by the crystal about his face and the company leaned in as he said seriously, "We may suppose them to be older than Merlin himself. As old as the great barrows and the stone circles. Long ago, before time was invented by men, we lived by the seasons, and could accurately predict eclipses and equinoxes. We moved between the realms of the living and the dead as easily as we now cross the street. These gifts are of an ancient knowledge which was closer then, than we are now, to understanding the nature of the universe, of the great questions of mankind and of God."

There was an awe-filled pause.

"Golly," said Caroline.

"Jolly old then," said her stupid husband with enthusiasm.

"Indeed," said the doctor.

The Captain, meanwhile, had resigned himself to his marooned state behind the curtain. His head had begun to nod and his yellow eyes closed in a long sleepy blink.

The conversation remained polite and revolved around the modest medium as the delicate soup bowls were replaced with delicate plates and they in turn were replaced with more delicate plates. This attrition saw the table's multitudes of china, crystal and silver dwindle as Mrs Potts' kitchen filled with empty and used utensils of every description. Little Lottie, the scullery maid, was activated in her primary purpose as she toiled at the deep sink, her arms plunged up to the elbows in hot greasy water.

Pausing with a diminutive spoon balanced between his thumb and forefinger, Mr Bingham savoured his mousse au chocolate and continued. "...so you believe, I take it Dr Connor, that each of us returns to earth after death to be re-incarnated?"

"You will recall, Mr Bingham, that the bible teaches us that 'God created man to be immortal; in the image of His own eternity created He him.' I myself have led many lives and have used my clairvoyant gifts in the service of my fellow man in each of them. When I was incarnated as the red Indian, *White Cloud,* I was able to lead my tribe to fertile hunting grounds. When I was a citizen of that great lost city of Atlantis I was able to create crystals for teaching purposes. If I may be immodest for a moment, I may say that King Arthur may have been defeated at Baden hill, but for my considerable intervention."

"Extraordinary," said Bingham as he tentatively attacked his mousse.

The young ladies around the table recalled the images they had seen of red Indians in their loin cloths. Countess Froud glowed. Lady Grasper wondered where Lionel might turn up next.

Mrs Potts ground the coffee beans in the managed chaos of the kitchen. Agnes mounted the stairs with delicate cakes. Haytor moved carefully with merlot, glistening in his stiff collar. Slink stooped to retrieve a wayward napkin. The Captain slept behind the curtain, his nose twitching in the food fragrant air as he dreamed of giblets.

In time, the dinner was completed and the servants were instructed to clear the table in readiness for the main event: The Séance. Mr Haytor blinked as Lady Grasper gave him instructions that he should personally ensure that the servants would remain below stairs. The ladies would not be withdrawing, for there was a meeting to take place following the dinner. If their services were required again she would ring for them.

"Very good your Ladyship," bowed Haytor as he withdrew and quietly closed the door, leaving the dinner guests to themselves.

"I must confess," giggled Freda, "that I have never taken part in a séance. I may say that I am rather nervous about it."

Dr Connor smiled benevolently and said, "You have my full assurance that the procedure of contacting the spirit world is as benign and satisfying as unexpectedly meeting an old acquaintance in the park."

Countess Froud looked worldly as she patted Freda's hand saying, "My dear girl, I myself was wary, I may even say sceptical of the experience. That is until I heard the voice of the dear Count." Her eyes became moist as she continued, "We are here for Lady Grasper, through Dr Connor we hope to channel our energy and contact the dear departed."

Freda seemed reassured so the doctor peered across the expanse of mahogany towards Lady Grasper. Dramatically, in the trenchant tones of a patient expert, he said, "Shall we begin?"

Lady Grasper nodded and shy Algernon gulped. The candles glowed about them as all eyes settled on the doctor. He took a deep breath and said, "Place your hands upon the table, thus."

They placed their hands, palms down on the mahogany. Freda giggled and received a stern look from her cousin, Fanny.

"Allow your fingers to touch those of the person next to you."

They allowed their fingers to touch. Freda giggled again and received a sterner look from Caroline.

"The circle is complete. I would like you all to close your eyes and try to imagine the candle flame in your mind."

They closed their eyes, and beneath the table, the experienced doctor felt with his foot for his home-made "knocking device." This, he always had hidden up his trouser leg for such events. In tremulous and dramatic voice he spoke.

"I call upon the ancestors, the ancient ones to act as our guides. Come forth so that our dearly departed may find their way to us from the other side."

With practiced care he used his foot to pull up his trouser leg, and poised the "knocking device" by the leg of his chair.

"I will ask you to knock to signal that you are there," he called out.

The Captain was at this precise moment in time, dreaming that he was stalking a large rat around the kitchen. The rat was sitting on its haunches, sniffing the air, and the Captain prepared to pounce. As he launched himself in his dream, in reality his back legs spasmed and rapped against the panelled wall by the window behind the curtain. The sudden report filled the room. An involuntary gasp issued forth around the table. Stoically, trusting in the supernatural skills of their leader, the dinner guests loyally sat with their eyes tightly shut. All, that is, except Dr Connor himself whose right eye furtively squinted around the room. His throat had suddenly become quite dry.

"Are you our spirit guide?" rasped the doctor uncertainly.

In the dream world which now tenuously encroached upon Dr Connors authority, the rat had broken free of the Captain's deathly grip and made a break for the scullery. The Captain launched himself at his adversary and unwittingly struck the panelling with a degree of force which half woke him. The sound seemed like a clap of thunder in the hushed, tense dining room. The rapid staccato pulse of his heart pounding in his ears, the doctor shut his eyes tightly at this second response. The Captain opened his. Perhaps it was a genuine psychic energy that was infused in the intrepid group of guests and made resonant by the Captain's unconscious rapping. Perhaps it was simply fate that it should happen at this precise moment. Whatever the reason, it was at this exact point in time that the Captain found his voice.

"Where am I?" he cried out as he looked around at his unfamiliar sleeping arrangement.

"It's Lionel!" squawked Lady Grasper. "I'd know his voice anywhere."

Still, they sat touching fingers; eyes clenched shut, breathing heavily but no, not as heavily as Dr Connor. His hyperventilation threatened to suck all vestige of oxygen from the room. His face was pallid beneath his quivering beard in strange defiance of his pounding heart. His eyes were no longer shut, they were gaping, they were straining, they rolled around in his head as he fought for his derelict composure. With quivering lips he tried to form words.

"Are you from the other side?" he rasped.

"Where am I, it's so dark?" cried out the Captain as, still sleepy, he arched and stretched his back.

"We're here Lionel, darling," choked Lady Grasper.

Dr Connor heard the scream fill the room. As everyone opened their eyes in shocked alarm, he became aware that they were looking at him in astonishment, and he realized to his added horror, that the scream was coming from him. He leaped to his feet and stumbled backwards, his knees clacking together uncontrollably. Indeed, his cunning "knocking device" made it seem as though he were wearing castanets in the manner of a one-man band. One leg of his trousers remained absurdly half-mast and revealed the squalid deception, strapped to his hairy white leg above his sock garter.

In moments like this, it is hard to predict what reaction may occur in polite society. In truth, the dinner party seemed frozen in time, their assembled expressions ranged from utter confusion (weak chinned Thomas) to stone faced incredulity (Lady Grasper). It was Countess Froud who moved first. She rose to her feet, trembling, not with fear but with a burning rage that only the hoodwinked can know. She took two paces and the other-worldly doctor found himself sitting on the carpet with the bold imprint of the aristocratic hand clearly discernable on the side of his face. There was language too, much language, as the doctor crawled on his hands and knees towards the door, the Countess helping him towards his sorry exit with well aimed kicks to his wizardly backside. The door opened before he could reach the handle and Mr Haytor surveyed the scene with a raised eyebrow. With great dignity, he said, "You rang your Ladyship?"

The disgraced Dr Conner was escorted unceremoniously to the door and ejected into the street, his hat thrown after him. He left town that night and was not seen in London again. The dinner guests comforted the distraught Countess, and felt themselves much ill used. The servants continued in their duties, shaking their heads. Only Lady Grasper was happy. She smiled as she visited her departed husband's study that night, for she was comforted that in her certain knowledge, it had been her dear clever Lionel who had interjected in the evening's drama on her behalf. It had been he who had exposed the fraud from beyond the grave. He was surely with her in spirit.

The Captain quietly slipped out of the dining room and returned unseen to below stairs, to the realm of industry, of servitude, and of the kitchen.

THE BLIND GIRL

The little girl was small, pale and thin. She had lived a sheltered life in a small terraced house in the East End of the big city. As long ago as she could remember, there had been stairs, and a loose, frayed piece of carpet. There had been a giggling game and then a tumble and the world had gone dark forever.

Today, on an autumn afternoon in 1940, she was carrying a small suitcase and attached to the button of her raincoat was a label. Upon it was written her name, and an address in a village far away in the countryside. She was not used to being out of her little house, but that morning a lady had arrived on the doorstep and had led her to a bus full of children. She could still hear her mother fussing as she left and then the unmistakable sound of her mother's sobs as she was led to the bus by the lady.

"Don't worry dear," the lady had said, "you're going to be safe, you'll see."

Her mother had returned to the little house having watched the bus drive away. She had seen her little girl sitting at the window, looking pale and afraid. Dazed, she had wandered into the parlour. She had looked at herself in the mirror over the mantelpiece where the clock ticked away the minutes. Arranged on the mantel were grey photographs of better times: the holidays by the sea in Devon; the family together at Christmas, wearing paper hats by the tree. Another picture was of her husband in uniform. He was in North Africa and it had been months since she had received his last letter home. She had looked again at the clock and fear had suddenly gripped her. An intuition. She had snatched up her bag in a moment of decision and ran into the street, not bothering to lock the door behind her. She had begun her race across the city to the station, where the trains always left on time.

The air was full of smoke, steam and whistles in the vast railway station. Beneath the great expanse of glass ceiling, blacked out to keep in the light, bustled all manner of people. There were people who were late, rushing with startled expressions along the platforms. There were people who were early, sitting on benches, staring at the large station clock, picking at their nails, killing time. There were soldiers in dull khaki, carrying their rationed belongings in strapped up backpacks. There were sailors who lingered, saying goodbye to their tearful wives and girlfriends. There were confident airmen, en-route to their airfields and spitfires. There were stoic policemen, directing anxious civilians to the tube station. And, in snaking chattering lines, there were throngs and throngs of children. The night before, more bombs had fallen on the embattled city, random incendiaries which had scorched and scarred houses, shops, and streets. The urgency was palpable among those who carried clipboards and crumpled notes. They were organizing the children into groups to board crammed train carriages that would carry them to the relative safety of rural England[*]. Many children, carrying their own diminutive luggage, had already been evacuated on the trains and the Captain had grown used to the sight.

The Captain had lived in the train station for as long as he could remember. He was entirely at home in the vast edifice of stone, ornate ironwork, and glass. He was unruffled amid the constant movement of locomotives and carriages, of people, baggage and parcels. He was calm amid the flux of comings and goings.

Amongst the hustle and bustle the Captain was a fixed constant. He knew all the best nooks for naps in surprisingly peaceful cupboards and stores. The porters and drivers, guardsmen and ticket collectors, the secretaries and signalmen, all knew the Captain. They always had time to give him a friendly smile and a pat. It was a dangerous time for the city and the Captain's presence provided a curious reassurance in this busy corner of it.

---

[*] Over 241,000 children were evacuated from London during the second world war to avoid the heavy German bombing campaign. Source: "Life in Wartime Britain" by Richard Tames. 1993.

Often he would visit his friend, the stationmaster, who had made a bed for him from a packing case in the corner of his office. Here they sat together and shared sandwiches and kippers. The Captain would curl up in his corner, listening to the sound of the stationmaster's voice as he gave instructions on his heavy black telephone behind his polished leather-topped desk.

At night, the Captain would climb high, high up to the very top of the great building and he would look up into the sky of winking stars and the old familiar face of the moon. Below, an infinite number of trains, trams, cars and buses toiled in the grim darkness of the blackout.

Heralded by the lament of wailing sirens, the flying machines would drone overhead and drop their senseless bombs. The Captain would flatten his ears and crouch low as he smelled the terrible odour of burning and watched the glowing sky. Despite the danger and destruction, the city and the station continued to keep the trains running on time in steady stubbornness. The smiles, pats, and shared kippers were unabated and defiant. The Captain and his station friends were on a war footing of a resilient, pragmatic, and undaunted English kind.

Autumn was bringing dark, chill afternoons to the grime encrusted streets. Today, inside the bright station, the Captain was sitting nonchalantly on an iron beam high above the people and the hissing trains. He was enjoying a cursory wash and half watching the snaking line of boys and girls arriving at the ticket collectors box. Wrapped in raincoats and wool, they carried their assortment of bags and teddy-bears, and waited to enter the long grey platform. Around each child's neck was a small, square box, containing a gas mask, and on their faces they wore a curious mixture of expressions: uncertainty, excitement, bewilderment, loss. They were guided by three ladies in tweed and at the rear of the meandering line one of the ladies led the little blind girl. The children stood fidgeting and squawking as the three ladies met the ticket inspector at the front of the line to organize the migration.

The little, pale, blind girl was disoriented and frightened by the strange noises and smells. She had never been in the big train station. She had never been on a train. She stood quietly in her tightly belted, oversized mackintosh, not knowing which direction to face. She felt her heart beating hard. She wanted to be home. When she felt the hand slip in hers she felt comforted and allowed herself to be led away.

From his high perch, the Captain watched, as the man led the girl briskly away from the platform. The man wore a flat cap pulled low over his face and he glanced back over his shoulder with a furtive, tight lipped intensity. The Captain could see beady eyes flickering from side to side so that it seemed to him that a giant rat was leading the girl urgently towards the station exit. They disappeared into the grey, milling crowd.

The Captain's leg was held aloft absent-mindedly in the middle of his wash. His eyes were fixed on the scene below as the ladies in tweed ran back and forth along the line of children calling out, "Esmerelda! Where are you, Esmerelda?"

People were walking by, carrying cases and packs, the women in tweed were talking to them and they were shaking their heads.

The Captain now trotted along the beam, high, high above the tracks. His eyes were dark and fixed on the exit far below as he glimpsed the rat man leading the girl outside into the evening.

The darkening, stone clad street was choked with tired and impatient people making their way home from the drudgery of their work. Despite the war, everything seemed strangely normal. Trams were laden with pallid commuters and at the corner of the street a red nosed man in fingerless woollen gloves was selling newspapers and bellowing, "Evening Standard, blackout murderer strikes again. Read all about it."

The watery sun was slipping behind the buildings; their haunted windows grew dark and sullen in their sooty façades.

High above the street, a black and white cat purposefully trotted along the top of the buildings. Pigeons sailed around his head, interrupted in their noisy, jostling, drama of roosting. The Captain seemed not to see them; he was looking down, as in the street below, the rat man led the little girl around the corner and out of sight.

The Captain cantered over the roof top. His yellow eyes were turning black and his white paws glowed in the twilight. Upon reaching the other side of the building he peered down and glimpsed rat man leading the girl across the road to an alley on the opposite side. The Captain raced toward the fire escape and with a twitch of his tail he started down the high ladder to the street below. The rungs were slippery and twice the Captain had to hang on for his life, his back legs reaching in the air, toes extended, to regain his perilous balance on the cold ladder rungs. Down, down he climbed and his whiskers bristled in the evening air as his paws touched the city paving. He was off at a gallop, deftly dodging in and out of the crowded pavement. A black taxicab swerved and screeched to a halt. He didn't hear the swearing driver as he sprinted across the busy street and down into the side alley.

The alley seemed strangely silent, empty, and removed from the city. The Captain trotted to the far end which opened into a quieter residential street, lined with rows of uniform grey houses. As the light was dimming, people were drawing their curtains to black out the light from within. There was no sign of the rat man or the little girl. The Captain trotted back through the alley and stopped. He closed his eyes and concentrated. He dipped his head, sniffed the pavement and smelled a thousand smells; a dizzying kaleidoscope of scent. Carefully, he moved across the width of the alley, sniffing here and there as his tail twitched in the air. His eyes were tightly shut as, trance-like, he slowly moved to and fro. He stopped and stiffened. He could see the station in his mind and, as he focused, the familiar smell of steam trains and the grimy whiff of the station floor revealed itself. Hoping against hope that the little girls' feet had laid the illuminating scent he carefully followed the trail to a small side door in the alleyway. He stood with his front legs on the step, whiskers twitching as he sniffed at the bottom of the door and then looked up. By this time it was becoming very dark, so that he could see from a chink of yellow light between grey curtains, that a sash window was open on the second floor.

Now, cats are renowned for their climbing ability, but most would not consider the possibility of scaling a brick wall to the height of a second storey window. The Captain had spent his life climbing in the railway station, and after all, he was a big cat. He crossed the alley and studied the side of the building and the window sill. Somewhere in the distance, above the drone of city noise, a horse whinnied. The Captain gathered himself and flexed his powerful thigh muscles. He took a deep breath and with all his strength and speed, he ran and leaped to the first floor window ledge. For a long, slow second, he coiled and compressed himself into a spring; there was a hush in a silent place, and then the spring's release: rocketing, twisting in the air, up to the window sill above. At full stretch he grabbed on with his front paws, his grappling hook claws biting into the paint-peeled wooden sill. His back legs raked against the hard brick where at last he found purchase amongst the crumbling mortar. Whiskers twitching, he hauled himself up onto the ledge.

He took a moment to catch his breath and then, very carefully, he dipped his head, peeping through the stained curtains into the room. He

76

was looking into a small cluttered kitchen lit by a single, yellowy, bare light bulb which hung from the ceiling by a short, plaited, discoloured wire. Beyond, was a dull brown painted door which stood ajar, and through it he could hear a child's voice asking, "When are we going to see my mum?"

The Captain swallowed and negotiated the soupy, stinking, sink under the window. With stealth he jumped down, being careful not to make a sound. He padded across the worn linoleum to the door and carefully looked into the room where the rat man stood with his back to him. The girl was sitting on the battered and greasy carcass of a settee in a dull, sparse, wall-papered, brown room that smelled of sewers and soiled sheets.

"Soon enough. You'll see your mum soon enough," the rat man said.

He was holding something in his hand and as the Captain watched, a knife blade appeared with a sharp click. The rat man walked over to the girl and bending, he cut the label from the button on her coat, crumpled it, and tossed it to one side. He closed the knife, easing the blade shut with the palm of his hand and slid it back into his pocket. The Captain's eyes grew dark as he watched the rat man walk around the girl with a brown-stained leer on his face. His beady eyes flickered under a mop of greasy hair as he reached out blackened stubby fingers and stroked the girl's cheek. She stiffened and recoiled in her seat. The Captain took a step back into the dim kitchen. He knew he must do something quickly. His mind was racing. He closed his eyes tightly as he tried to think. Out of a distant past flickered a recollection: an image like a faded photograph; a smiling old man in front of a small round house. He opened his eyes again, swallowed, and found his loudest voice,

"The train now leaving from platform 8 is the 10.49 bound for Bristol."

He sensed the man spin around and heard a gruff bark. "Who's there? Who's that?"

The Captain shrunk back into the corner of the kitchen; he heard the click of the knife at it sprang open. He saw the shadow of the rat man half crouched, looming, stealthy and dangerous at the doorway.

"The train now arriving at platform 9 is the 6.55 from Horsham," announced the Captain.

He saw the man's hand and the knife that it clasped, then his glinting beady eyes looking in. The Captain was careful to hide his white face and cloaked himself in his black fur, not daring to move or breathe.

The man slowly moved into the kitchen.

"Who's that? You'll be sorry when I cut ya'."

Frowning, he looked about him and seeing no one he went to the window. Cautiously, he opened the fluttering curtains and standing to one side, he craned his neck to look up and down the alley. Seeing nothing, he drew the curtains apart, opened the sash to its full height, and leaned out to look up and down the street. The Captain was waiting for his moment and rat man leaned out just a little bit more. Too late did he hear the acceleration of claws and clatter across the scarred linoleum. The Captain launched himself at the man's back with all his weight and might, and with the same powerful hind legs that he had used to come in through the window, he now propelled the rat man out of it. There was a crunch below, a pause, and then a yelp.

"I've broken me bloody leg. Me bloody legs are busted."

The Captain hopped onto the sill and looked down to see rat man sprawled on his back in the alley. Then he turned, jumped down, and trotted to the girl.

"Esmerelda," he said.

"Who's there?" asked the girl uncertainly.

"Oh, I'm just a friend who came to take you back to a safe place. I'm here with my pet cat. Would you like to stroke him?"

The girl nodded. The Captain came closer and allowed the girl to run her fingers through his thick coat. "I have an idea," he said. "You hang onto my old cat's tail and we'll leave this smelly place and go to find your mum."

The girl stroked his fur and in a small voice said, "Alright."

It was an unusual sight for those pale commuters in the dark streets who glimpsed the Captain leading the girl back to the station. Even the newspaper seller grew quiet as he watched. When they arrived back among the bustle and chuffs, the whistles and echoes, the Captain felt the girl's hand grip his tail more tightly.

"Don't worry," he said softly.

The station was busier than usual with policemen. The ladies in tweed were still there, wringing their hands and looking flustered. The stationmaster was talking to them and wearing an uncharacteristic frown. He was trying to comfort another lady with a tear-stained face who clutched her bag tightly with anxiety.

That great building was rarely quiet, was rarely hushed, but quiet and hushed it became. The people forgot the time and stopped bustling. They stopped and stepped back; they stood and stared in quizzical silence as the Captain led the little girl across the vast expanse of station floor. The ladies in tweed sighed in relief and the stationmaster beamed as the Captain guided the little blind girl back into the arms of her teary, grateful mother.

No one was ever able to explain what had happened that evening. It seemed to be a collection of unrelated events. Who was the stranger who had spoken to the little girl and returned her? How was it that a known criminal came to be lying in an alley with a murder weapon and a broken leg? (That night he ended up in the prison hospital at Pentonville. He was going to do time). It was thought a lucky chance that the girl had grabbed the tail of the station cat and only natural that the cat would have found the stationmaster. A reporter came and the two were photographed together for the Evening Standard. The following day the picture appeared under the joke headline:

STATION CAT FINDS MISSING GIRL!

Some kind people who read the newspaper article forwarded an invitation, and the little blind girl left London with her mum to live in a large and comfortable house on the coast. The stationmaster read the news aloud to the Captain as they shared their kippers together and the Captain blinked his large yellow eyes.

THE RETURN

Clay sat in the motorway service station restaurant on an immovable chair. In front of him was a plastic plate and he nudged at his potato wondering if it was genetically modified. He turned back to his briefing notes which were headed with the words: *your eyes only*. As an archaeologist he wasn't used to this melodrama. He re-read the notes and the sick feeling in his stomach returned. Not the food this time. He checked his wristwatch, put the notes back into his briefcase, and walked towards the car-park; past the rows of bleeping arcade machines and through the glass doors into the hot, fumes-sweetened air. He followed directions to the motorway ramp and drove his battered Focus north for about three miles before pulling onto the hard shoulder, tumbling from the car and throwing up.

The site was surrounded by a high fence topped with razor-wire. A second fence was under construction and ditches were being dug by machines that rumbled back and forth on caterpillar tracks. Outside the fence were encampments of protestors and a vandalized visitor's centre extolling the virtues and modern necessity of the new missile shield and its defensive capability. Soldiers were sweating and hard at work in the unusual spring heat, removing graffiti and repairing information boards. Inside the fence, the press corps was touring the site in golf carts with a ministry spokesman. They proceeded along newly laid concrete pathways that linked the planned missile complex. A military presence was on hand *24/7*, they were being told, to ensure public safety and to mitigate any disturbance of construction crews by undesirables.

"You know, this project will provide much needed employment for local people. The American base alone is expected to create one hundred and fifty full and part-time jobs in the catering and ancillary industries."

"Ancillary?"

"Yes, you know, cleaning and so on. Of course, everyone will be properly screened."

"What is the current budget for construction?"

"I'm sorry; I'm not in a position to give out that information at this time."

"How many missiles will actually be deployed here when the site is finished?"

"I'm sorry; you will appreciate that that is classified information at this time."

The newspaper reporter glanced up at the hill and the ancient tree which stood at the heart of the site.

"What about the Druid hill, what are the plans for that?"

"You know, we're very aware of the sensitivity surrounding the landmark and any work around the hill will be with the full consultation of professional archaeologists."

Clay took his exit from the motorway and arched his back away from the plastic seat. His shirt was stuck to him with sweat and his hands were sticky on the steering wheel. He slowed his speed and wound down the window, taking deep breaths and fumbling with his map. He pulled over and the car idled as he traced his route with his finger; the blue lines of the motorway; the red line of the connector; the grey line of the Roman road. He followed it with his eye, its culmination in the words *ancient landmark*. Confident that he had his bearings, he folded the map, checked his mirror and started to pull away, immediately slamming on the brake. A stag stood in the road watching him through the windscreen, its eyes peering into his. Very still. Clay heard his pulse thumping in his ears. Time seemed to slow. He checked his wristwatch. He was late. Looking up again, the animal was gone. He wiped his face with his sleeve, put the car into gear and pulled away, flicking on the radio:

"We're reporting record temperatures again today and the outlook shows that there is more of this fine weather on the way. Health authorities are urging the public to drink plenty of liquids and don't forget that sunscreen! And now, more uninterrupted soft favourites..."

He hummed as he drove. Pulling onto the Roman road he could see the hill in the distance and he thought again of the cottage for sale in Southern France.

He arrived at the double gates of the security checkpoint and showed the guard the identity card that had been issued to him by the Ministry of Defence. The guard waved him through and pointed towards the portable administration building. He parked his Focus in the spot marked "visitor" and climbed the steps to reception. Inside, the hiss of air-conditioning reminded him of gas leaks. Behind the faux wood reception desk a young woman in military uniform was talking on a headset and typing on a keyboard at the same time. Clay waited awkwardly for her to finish and shivered as his sweat soaked shirt cooled in the air-conditioned temperature. He was thinking of the first time he had visited the hill with its ancient tree. He had been a passionate archaeology student with a fascination for the Neolithic. How times change.

"Sir, can I help you?"

She was looking at him with impatience. He realized that his mind had wondered.

"Ah yes, let me see now," he said as he fumbled with a damp envelope folded in his trouser pocket. She tapped her finger nail on her desk as he tore the letter in his hurry to open it. He smiled at her and she looked back with a deadpan face.

"I'm here to see Colonel Nettles."

"Name?"

He blinked. "Colonel Nettles," he said again.

"Your name."

"Sorry, stupid of me, I'm Dr Clay from Oxford University."

"Please take a seat."

He sat, perched on a soft vinyl covered bench as he drank water from a disposable paper cup. Flicking through the glossy missile shield brochure, he read:

In our modern world we face many real threats from weapons of mass destruction. Apart from appropriate strike intervention, the NATO missile shield is our best defence against terror states which continue to develop their own missile technologies.

"Dr Clay," said the Colonel in his neat, pressed uniform. Smiling, he extended his hand. Clay wiped his hand on the side of his crumpled trousers and the two men shook.

"Please come through."

Clay followed him down a short corridor and into an office that smelled of citrus air freshener where the Colonel sat behind a large desk. Maps and diagrams covered the walls. Clay sat in the offered chair.

"I hope you had a pleasant drive down. Great weather out there. No trouble from protests at the gate I hope."

"No, no trouble at all."

"Good, good. Coffee?"

"No, thank you."

"You've had plenty of time to read through your briefing notes I hope."

"Yes."

"Any outcomes?"

"I'm sorry?"

"I trust it all made sense."

"Yes."

"Good, good. Look, Dr Clay, I won't beat around the bush, you know we have a sticky PR problem here?"

"Yes, I realize that."

"Well, we drafted you in because you're the authority on these old places."

"The Druid hill."

"Exactly. The problem is that the hill has to be modified. Ground penetrating radar suggests that it's hollow."

"Annwn."

"I beg your pardon?"

"In legend it is an entrance to Annwn, the Otherworld."

"Well, you've read the briefing notes. We have to stabilize it with landfill and flatten the top for our communications array."

"Yes, I read that."

"We need you on site to explain that no damage will be incurred in the modification. The hill will still be there after all."

"Yes."

"Good. And you're happy with the compensation package we prepared for you?"

"It's very generous."

"Excellent."

Clay grew awkwardly flustered and stammered as the reality sunk in. He said, "And...and the tree. The tree will be removed to the Natural History Museum?"

"That was a great suggestion of yours and of course, the work will be carried out under your direction."

"It's been carbon dated at over two thousand years old."

"Well, do what you need to do. Your ID gives you full access. I'm glad we have you on side, Dr Clay. We've booked you a room at The Lightning Tree Inn at the village. Charge everything you need to our account."

The Colonel was standing, extending his hand again. Clay's ears were ringing as he left.

"When I'm calling yoooou,ooooh,oh,oooh,ooh,ooooh,ooh...I will answer you, oooh,ooh,oooooh,oooh,ooh..."

The keeper lady sang along to the crackling radio in her warbling voice as she swept the linoleum floor. Impassively, the Captain watched from his cage. She looked up and smiled at him from under her blue rinse hair. "Listening to the nice song, Scotty?" she quavered as she gripped the plastic dustpan. He blinked and settled back into silent thought. He was imbued with an unconscious knowledge that straddled two thousand years: a legacy of lives lived. There were moments when an image would appear in his head without explanation and without reference, so that as he sat in meditation, peering into the half distance, his mind became a magic lantern of random imagery. Sometimes, the pictures would be triggered by a familiar word, half heard on the crackling radio. This did not create confusion for him; he didn't attempt to make sense out of the chaos of his memory, but rather he regarded the images from a distance, without prejudice, without longing. It was the observation of disconnected philosophical elegance that only a cat could understand, especially one of the Captain's deep and mysterious experience. After all the history, the life and death, he now found himself locked in a cage among many others in a small white room which whined with fluorescent lighting. As he sat, hour upon hour, and day upon day, week upon week and month after month, the flickering images became all that he had. People would come and go with the keeper ladies, and the cats in all the other cages, piled up upon one another would come and go too. When people came into the room the other discarded cats would rouse themselves and cry out to advertise their presence. The people would coo and touch the bars of the cages and point to a cat and it would be removed from its cage with ceremony and taken away from the whining room in a cardboard carrying box. While all this activity was taking place, the Captain remained curled up, cloaked, and disinterested. He was too old for adoption so that without the appeal of youth or kitten-hood, he remained disenfranchised from the trees, grass and fields that he loved.

His friend, a retired professor, had sold their little house in Glastonbury and moved them north to be close to his daughter and her new family. The apartment that he had bought was sold when the professor couldn't take care of them anymore; his mind had crumbled over time and he no longer recognized the Captain. The daughter was afraid that the old cat might hurt her new baby; not out of malice, but perhaps from some pathogen. She was afraid of germs which she had read about in *Family Monthly*. Her husband was sad to take the old cat to the shelter, just as he had been sad to take his father-in-law to the old people's home. He told himself that this was for the best.

It was growing dark and the keeper lady was preparing to leave; glancing at the clock. "Good heavens, is that the time?" The radio crackled with static as she moved around, checking the cages for feed and water. A reedy oboe was broadcasting from London. She flicked off the lights and closed the door.

*"Time now for the six o'clock news. There is further controversy tonight over the government decision to house the national missile defence shield base in an area which protestors say...*crackle, crackle... *national importance. The site, which includes the so-called Druid hill, has had calls in the past...*crackle...*A government spokesman said today that work to build the missile site will be sensitively handled and will include an archaeological assessment by the eminent scholar, Dr Robert Clay. The spokesman added that the site is in an ideal and strategically important position and that national security must trump...*crackle...*President praised the decision. In other news..."*

The Captain sat with his head on one side listening. A single memory of a tree on a hill now crystallized in his head and he sat up in his cramped cage. The words came to him.

"Leaf," he cried out in the twilight, "LEAF, LEAF, LEAF."

Three thousand miles away, she opened her dark eyes.

Clay was wasting no time. His orders were to move quickly. The protests were growing; more campers were arriving every day and the public relations people were telling him that things could get ugly. His first day had been spent with a work crew digging at the hard ground beneath the great tree. They had resorted to jack-hammers as they cut into the hill, removing the earth, smashing through unyielding roots as tough as iron. The tree was braced and held now by wire cables as they worked at weakening the root-ball to enable them to wrench the tree from the ground. It would happen tomorrow. Though weathered and eroded, the tree still impressed Clay with its remarkable bulk; reverently he touched it with his hand and wondered at the history it must have seen. Then he felt a rush of excitement at the prospect of its removal and his subsequent dig into the hill. His heart pounded with the potential of what may lie beneath. He remembered the treasures recovered from the hills at Sutton Hoo in East Anglia. Perhaps there were burial chambers, artefacts. And the tree would look grand in the foyer of the museum. The director there had been excited by the prospect. Then he shrugged, what did he care anymore?

That night, Clay sat in his room at the inn, writing his report on his laptop. He was describing the delicate process that had been required to dig down through the roots of the Lightning Tree. He wrote that the process had been fortunate, timely—he had found serious decay. He wrote that the tree's removal was the only way to save it from collapse; that this presented an opportunity to explore beneath the tree, to re-examine some of the myths of the place and to enrich our knowledge as archaeologists. He sat back, pleased with himself. If he played his cards right he might get a fat grant to write a paper on this. He wiped his face with his handkerchief and stretched his back. It was still hot. He sauntered to the open window and looked out into the still night. The waxing moon illuminated the countryside and he could see the hill in the distance, beyond the rumbling by-pass. The dark shape of the tree stood alone there. Clay was surprised by the emotion that caught him in the throat for a moment. *Your last night on the hill*, he thought to himself. A fox barked in the distance.

The Witch of Nu was wrapped in her cloak as she flew towards London at forty thousand feet. She adjusted her dark, wire rimmed sunglasses as she looked down upon the world and curled her long hand around the pouch that she wore at her neck. She sat alone in the jump seat of the special charter cargo jet. Nearby, braced and tethered in the cavernous space, was the large travelling crate that had been loaded by sweating porters in Addis Ababa. Inside, the great black horse was silently waiting. On the flight deck, the crew were discussing the strange nature of their assignment and the possible identity of their sole passenger. They could not, in their wildest imagination, have guessed the truth. The hair was greying now but the power was undiminished. She was the last but one of the great ancients. Captain Gillespie handed responsibility to his co-pilot and made his way aft. It was strangely cold back there. He approached the woman uncertainly, unable to explain the nervousness he felt as he looked at her, sitting so very still in the half-light. He felt the horse watching him through the grating of the crate.

"Anything we can get for you, madam?"

She turned her head slowly, and he saw himself reflected in her impenetrable glasses. He swallowed as she answered in a quiet voice. "I have everything I need, thank you."

Clay had not slept well. He now sat in front of his cold, fried breakfast and managed to drink half a cup of coffee. He checked his wristwatch and then drove to the site. As he approached, he could see through the gates that the huge crane was ready. He slowed at the security check-point and his Focus was pelted with eggs by the protestors who were yelling, held back behind police lines. He was waved through quickly and within an hour was directing activity. The crane swung its huge boom into position and cast a gallows shadow across the hill. His stomach churned as he watched the crew securing the great hook of the crane around the girth of the tree. Many from the offices had come to watch the operation, ignoring the chants of protestors beyond the fence:

"Hands off the Lightning Tree...Hands off the Lightning Tree...Hands off the Lightning Tree."

Clay looked around and Colonel Nettles gave him a nod. He was smiling. Clay gave the signal to proceed and the workers retreated as the huge crane took up the slack of the immense reinforced steel cable. The tree shuddered as the cable tightened and the cranes outriggers bit into the scarred ground. Clay wanted to stop it, a voice in his head was screaming for him to stop it. He didn't move as he clenched his hands tightly together, feeling his nails biting into his flesh. He wanted to close his eyes. He could hear the protestors screaming from beyond the fence. The boom of the crane was straining as the cable was slowly wound in. Clay was talking to himself.

"What's keeping it in the ground? Give in, for heaven's sake, give in."

The strain seemed impossible and then there was an indescribable tearing sound as the tree let go of the earth. It bounced for a moment and then swayed in the air like a hanged man. The weight of its branches inverted it as the earth's gravity demanded its return so that it dangled, pathetically, upside down. The work crew was cheering and the protestors were fighting with the police as Clay looked up.

"I'm sorry," he whispered.

In his cage, the Captain felt that his heart was breaking. The keeper lady tried to console him as he cried.

The tree was swung aside and lowered onto a huge flatbed lorry as Clay peered into the gaping hole that had been left in the hill. Excitement gripped him as he saw a perfectly cut, stone spiral staircase that descended into the earth. He clambered down, marvelling at the workmanship. At a depth of twenty feet, the staircase disappeared below a massive sarcen stone. He felt with his shaking fingers, the incredible way the stone had been cut to fit the staircase. It reminded him of the building work at the five thousand year old settlement at Skara Brae in Scotland. He tried to imagine what could possibly be down there. He climbed back up and was greeted by Colonel Nettles who held out his hand.

"Congratulations, Dr Clay,"

"This is an extraordinary... a very exciting find," said Clay, indicating the staircase.

"Just remember why you're here," hissed the Colonel as he looked him in the eye and jabbed his finger hard in his chest.

Clay felt his face reddening. "Yes, of course."

The Colonel regarded him closely for a moment, then turned and left him standing there, on the damaged hill. Clay determined to spend the rest of the day in examination of the tree and in the preparations for its removal to London.

Several of its branches had split under the tree's own weight as it had been lowered onto the flatbed. Clay was surprised at how hollow the tree was. As it lay there on its side, he was able to climb through its torn root system and stand up. An inspection of the interior puzzled him, and he spent several hours with a hammer and chisel, recovering silver disks that seemed almost to have grown out of the wood. When he was satisfied that he had recovered them all, it was growing late in the afternoon. He looked up at the hill and decided to climb to the summit again. The air was still as he climbed. He passed the orange lines that had been spray-painted onto the grass to mark the coming excavation. He looked into the hole, at the extraordinary stone staircase and to the bottom. He was nodding to himself. Tomorrow he was determined to break through with the jack-hammers.

A cold breeze on his neck surprised him and he turned to see the southern sky darkening with storm clouds.

"Hello, something's blowing in," he said to himself.

As he retraced his steps down the hill, the warm day evaporated and darkness fell. The sun was obliterated by the gathering clouds, its disk of light hung blindly at the rim of the world and then it slid away. By the time he reached his car, chilled darkness had enveloped him and flecks of snow were melting on the still warm ground. He drove past the blue flashing lights of the police cars at the gate and headed for the village.

He arrived back at the inn, gladdened by its glowing windows as he shivered across the car-park in his thin jacket, clutching his heavy briefcase, stuffed with silver disks.

"I didn't pack for this weather," he muttered to himself.

Inside, the locals were sipping their beer and sitting around the television set on the wall. There was *news just in* of the ice storm that was sweeping across the continent and they sat with incredulous faces voicing loud opinion. The weather centre was announcing freak conditions to come and it suspected climate change as the cause. Temperatures were expected to plummet and authorities were advising people to stay indoors and not to travel unless absolutely necessary.

The cargo jet touched down on the icy runway. Captain Gillespie's jaw was knotted as he felt the plane slide for a moment before de-accelerating. Even in the darkness what he saw about him was shocking. Everything was clad in thick ice. London airport had become an ice sculpture. The storm had propelled them along for much of the flight and its first wave had swept past them as they had approached the UK. There was more on the way. They taxied across the frozen tarmac and the engines whined to a halt in the bright neon light at the gate. The customs official was stamping his feet in the cold and gripping his clipboard with numbed fingers as the huge cargo door opened. He peered into the enormous cavity and then staggered backwards as the black horse walked down the ramp, ridden by the Witch of Nu.

"You can't ride that animal, it will have to be quarantined," said the official as he squinted at his paperwork. Looking up again, his jaw became slack as the witch put on her helmet. She looked about her, removed her glasses and swept back her cloak, revealing her armour of chain mail and glinting breastplate. The official covered his eyes when she looked at him and then she spurred her horse and rode out, leaving mangled security fences in her wake.

Motorways and roads had become clogged by abandoned vehicles and the ice had brought down power lines, plunging much of the country into darkness. It was as though Britain had been thrown back in time. People huddled together in their homes in the cities, towns and villages. Engines seized and ceased to work as it became colder and colder. All aircraft were grounded and a state of emergency was announced by authorities. The Prime Minister appealed for calm as he spoke on television until that too became black.

The witch travelled overland throughout the night. Under the bright moon she cantered across frozen rivers and through housing estates. She traversed silent motorways and thundered through train tunnels. She passed industrial parks and big-box stores; galloped through recreational grounds and urban centres. All the while, she carried her round shield, the image of a tree upon it.

The keeper lady had walked to the cat shelter in the freezing morning. She wasn't expecting anyone to come by, but the cats had to be fed. The dry meal clattered into plastic dishes as she listened to the emergency channel on the radio. It was telling people what to do and what not to do in the frigid temperatures. Apparently, the Siberian conditions were, without question, the worst on record. The keeper lady tut-tutted as she listened and filled the old paraffin heater. The Captain heard the hooves on the icy road outside. The keeper lady was trying to tune in the radio as it went off like a Geiger counter. The door opened and the witch, swathed in her cloak, came into the room.

"Hello dear, I wasn't expecting anyone today," said the keeper lady, squinting at her guest.

The cats were strangely quiet as the witch looked around at the cages. The Captain sat up as he watched her and felt his mind clearing and coming into focus. His memories were flooding back and they now arranged themselves in a seamless chronology, filling him with the power of his experience. The witch was watching him and smiled as she pointed toward his cage.

"I've come for him, for the Captain," she said.

The keeper lady furrowed her brow. "Are you sure, dear? He's very old you know."

"So am I," she replied.

"Well, well. Lucky old Scotty. Let me go and find a carrying box."

"That isn't necessary, thank you."

With that, she took from her shoulder, the preserved carpet bag of Hugh de Paynes and the Captain cried out. She opened the cage and he curled himself around her neck before climbing into the familiar bag. Within, he found flecked upon its interior, his own black and white fur of an earlier existence. He began to purr.

A tracked troop carrier had been sent to pick up Clay and he rode inside it from the inn back to the site. He was dressed in a motley assortment of borrowed military clothes to survive the weather. He had been told there had *been a development* and he felt anxious about the implication. At the gate, he saw that the visitors centre had been turned into a shelter for the protestors who seemed uncharacteristically exuberant. They were warming their hands, gathered around improvised fires in steel drums. They were shaking their heads and grinning. Inside the compound, Colonel Nettles was waiting, grim faced, as Clay climbed from the growling vehicle.

"Is there a problem?" Clay asked nervously.

In response, Nettles indicated the hill with a jerk of his head. Clay turned and blinked. Upon the hill stood a huge oak tree. He looked at the parked flatbed, the Lightening Tree still lay there, just as he had left it.

"I don't understand," he said.

"Just get this figured out before the press get hold of it," snapped Nettles. "I want a report and action plan on my desk by the end of the day."

Clay could hear his breath crackle in the freezing air as he climbed the hill. His brain felt numb as he thought of the legend of the hill, of Annwn. He approached the tree uncertainly, asking himself: *What does this mean? What does this mean?* The tree was unquestionably alive. It seemed to grow out of the hole that the Lightning Tree had occupied. Clay took a deep breath as he looked at it. It was impossible. It was a phenomenon. His mind felt woollen, he couldn't think. He touched the bark of the vast trunk. It was easily the largest tree that he had ever seen but where the heck had it come from? How, how?

"What does this mean?"

Under the leaden sky, the black horse trekked across the silent land. In the distance, wisps of smoke curled in the air as people lit fires to keep warm. The witch and the Captain now talked together. It had been he who had opened her eyes with his call from his cage and he wondered where this journey might end. He didn't want bloodshed. He knew of her power, of her capability and he pleaded for time, for a chance to avert her wrath. He invoked the memory of the old man, the Druid of Môn, and she listened to him. They came to an agreement.

For the time being, work around the site had halted. The soldiers were helping local farmers get feed to their animals and assisting the village inhabitants. The PR people thought that this would be a good idea. A satellite link had been established and news was trickling in of the extent of the ice storms damage. If conditions continued for very long, it was thought that millions could die. People were panicking. Food, fuel and water were being looted from shops and supermarkets. Pipes were frozen. The police were losing their grip on the situation and the towns and cities were turning into no-go zones.

Clay sat once more in the office of Colonel Nettles. He had no explanations, no action plan.

"Do you have any idea what's at stake here, Clay?" Colonel Nettles was red in the face and angry. He hadn't been sleeping well. He was having bad dreams. He had woken himself with a scream. He was hanging on.

Clay didn't know what to say. He shrugged.

"A great deal of money, that's what," continued Nettles, "let alone the security of NATO. I want that tree out of there. I don't care how it got here, get it out before the press get hold of it."

"I think it's something very special," mumbled Clay.

"Have it cut down, do you hear me? Get rid of it. I'll assign a team to help you in the morning, now get out."

Clay rose from his chair and quietly walked to the door.

"Clay."

Clay turned.

"Don't cross me. You'll be sorry if you cross me."

Clay fumbled with the handle and left.

He felt sick as he rumbled back to the inn within the belly of the troop transport vehicle. Later, he poked at the fish-fingers on his plate and worried about their mercury content. He thought again of the cottage for sale in Southern France and looked at the estate agents flyer that he carried in his wallet. So much seemed to have happened in so short a time, his dream now seemed to exist in another world. He thought about the stag that he had seen on the road. It felt like a thousand years ago. In an attempt to calm his mind he played solitaire until it was time for bed and then he stretched out and closed his eyes, hoping for sleep, dreading what the next day may bring.

Outside, in the freezing night, a black horse cantered along the Roman road.

In the early hours of the morning, Colonel Nettles whimpered. He was having the dream again:

The woman with the black eyes, smiling at him; he was standing on the hill looking down at the gaping hole in his chest; he saw that she held something in her bloody hand; holding it to show him — his own beating heart.

Clay, too, was sleeping. The room was silent but for the dull tick of his digital alarm clock. Something was sitting on his bed in the darkness. He half woke, feeling the pressure against his leg. He murmured for a moment as it shifted and then his eyes opened wide in fear. He lay still, hardly daring to breathe or move, feeling the weight on the bed. His pulse hammered in his ears. Very slowly, he began to move his arm. He groped in the darkness for the torch on the bed-side table. Closing his fingers around it, he held it up. He took a deep breath and pressed the button. The cat was staring back at him, its eyes glowing in the light beam like silver disks.

"Wake up, Robert Clay," said the Captain.

Clay tried to form words as he fought to keep control of his bladder. His hand was shaking violently as he held the torch.

"I am here to council you," continued the Captain. "You have placed yourself in great danger."

Clay closed his eyes and opened them again. The cat was still there.

"Please take me seriously," said the Captain.

Clay realized that he had stopped breathing and gasped for air.

"What are you?" he managed to croak.

"I am the messenger of the Witch of Nu."

"This isn't happening."

"I can assure you, Dr Clay, that this is very real."

Clay's mind was numb but his initial terror had begun to subside. He sensed that the animal was not going to hurt him. He wondered if he had finally cracked. "Am I insane?" he squeaked.

"Remember when you were a little boy? You were digging in the garden and you found an arrowhead of flint."

"I remember."

"And what did you do?"

"I...I...

"You put it in your catapult and fired at the squirrel."

Clay spoke in a choked voice. "I didn't mean to. I didn't mean to...kill it."

"We are responsible for our actions. Tears will not bring back the dead but we can make atonement for our mistakes. Work must stop on the hill. The fences must be removed; the damage must be repaired."

Clay began to weep. His nightmare was fully formed. "What can I do about it?" he squeaked again.

"You can do your job. You're on the wrong side of the protest line."

Clay's shoulders began to shake and he tried to wipe away tears. The Captain watched him. *Will this man ever wake up?* He spoke again.

"Have you ever contemplated your own death? Ever wondered how it will happen? Trust me, it will happen soon unless you act."

Clay blinked. "No one can stop them. This is the government, big business, NATO. It's impossible."

"I say to you again, Dr Clay, that work must stop. If you do not act, the Witch of Nu will. She protects the Otherworld and has destroyed armies; crushed empires in its defence. She will snuff you out with a glance."

Clay shook his head. "I can't stop it. It's impossible."

"Anything is possible. Let me remind you that you are having a conversation with a cat."

Clay chuckled as a surge of hysteria swept through his mind. "A witch's cat," he sniggered.

The Captain spat and hissed at him, "Let me put this in a way that you can understand. I have launched the ultimate weapon and she is here. She sleeps in the earth, is part of the earth and she is awake. She is the fulcrum; if challenged she will annihilate you. You think it's cold now? She can bring an ice-age that will bury you. *Bury you.* Do you understand?"

Clay's eyes were wide. His lips trembled. The Captain softened his voice. "My teacher once told me that if I use words wisely, with discretion, and with a good heart, I will be like the brightest star in the sky. You must now raise your voice, Robert Clay."

Clay sat very quietly and wiped his nose on his pyjama sleeve.

"Tell me what you want me to do," he said.

"Get dressed."

Ten minutes later, Clay stood nervously in the car-park looking up at the black horse and its surreal rider. The Captain was curled upon her shoulder and whispered into her ear. She looked at Clay with her green eyes and offered her long hand. He reached up uncertainly and she took his arm, nearly wrenching it from its socket as she swung him onto the horse behind her.

"Hold tight," said the Captain.

Clay hung on to the witch's waist and squeezed his eyes tightly shut as they took off. He could feel the cold air biting at his face as they moved across the icy landscape, across the fields and the silent by-pass towards the site.

The witch brought them to a dark spot near the gate and dropped them off as dawn glimmered in the distance. Clay wore the carpet bag over his shoulder and the Captain looked from it at the witch.

"You will return the sun?"

She smiled and nodded. "I'll be watching," she said and rode away.

At the gate, the security guard examined Clay's ID pass, nodded and let them through.

"First, there is someone I want you to meet," said the Captain and together they climbed the hill. True to the witch's word the dawn revealed a clear sky and as they reached the tree on the hill, the sun once more began to glow at the horizon. The Captain climbed up into the tree and nuzzled against it.

"My old friend," whispered the Treeman.

Clay watched as the branches moved, lightly stroking the cat. This was the oldest living ancient, come to straddle the hill-top in defiance of any who would try to move him.

"Speak to him," said the Captain. "Tell him what he has done."

Clay trembled as the tree man fixed him with a gnarled and knotted eye.

"You have endangered the world. You have stopped listening. You have forgotten who you are."

"Tell him what he must do," said the Captain.

"You must open your eyes. You must respect where you come from. You must repair the damage."

The Treeman spoke to the Captain again. "Dear old friend, tell me, are you here to visit or to return?"

"To return," said the Captain."

"Ah, then we will be together again. I know of an old man who will welcome you home."

They left the Treeman and climbed back down the hill in the red glow of the dawn. With the Captain hidden inside the carpet bag, Clay now set to work at a desk, writing to every contact he had. He wrote, with a passion he thought he had lost, of the enormous significance of the hill in Celtic mythology. He wrote of the need to preserve it for future generations. He wrote that an irreplaceable part of Britain was being destroyed. He denounced the plans as government sanctioned vandalism. He was finishing uploading his work on the satellite link when Colonel Nettles arrived.

"Here nice and early, I see. Good, good. Now get to work on that tree. The work detail is waiting outside."

"Go and stick your missiles where the sun don't shine."

Nettles' face froze. "What?" he barked.

"Did you know I went to university with the Prime Minister? I've emailed him to tell him that this base is a disaster in every sense and that if he wants to preserve a shred of public support, he'd better start looking at alternatives."

Nettles looked incredulous.

"You're a dead man, Clay."

"I was dead, but I've woken up."

"Get out there and cut that tree down."

Clay looked him in the eye. "No."

Nettles, crazed with anger, stormed out. They heard orders being shouted and from the window, Clay saw Nettles leading the workmen up the hill with chainsaws.

"We have to stop them," snapped the Captain.

The guard at the security gate was expecting another quiet day as work at the site had been delayed. He sat in his cubicle reading "Moby Dick." He shook his head, Captain Ahab was going mad. The sound of galloping hooves made him look up in puzzlement. He glimpsed a flashing blade, a fountain of flame and sparks, and the gates fell in half. A frothing black horse hammered past him. He hit the alarm button and the soldiers in the garrison scrambled into action.

The witch swept up the hill, the curved blade of her sword trailing in her hand like a glinting claw. She thundered past the work team and her great black horse reared with a menacing scream as she arrived at the summit. The Captain too, pounded to the top and climbed into the arms of the Treeman who himself was prepared to do battle if necessary. He shook his great limbs as the work team watched in disbelief. Clay thought he would black out as he ran hard in pursuit and behind him, with automatic weapons, came the paratroops. Colonel Nettles stood with a look of confusion on his face as the witch now approached him on her snorting horse at a walk, her eyes darkening, becoming black. The crew threw away their chainsaws and ran, tumbled away. Nettles couldn't move. He was rooted to the spot as the terror gripped him.

"Remember me?" said the witch quietly. "I've come to rip out your heart and send you to burning hell."

Nettles buckled and fell to the ground, sobbing. The paratroops knelt in firing position, squinting through their gun sights, their fingers resting on their triggers. They took nervous aim and focused on the ancient breastplate as it sparkled in the morning sun. Their magnified vision revealed its swirling filigree, its delicate tracery, forming rivers in their minds, and for a quivering moment, the fate of humanity lay within the clinch of a soldier's finger. Then they were blinded by orange. Clay stood gasping in front of them with arms splayed in his borrowed arctic parka.

"Stop," yelled Clay standing with his back to the witches stamping horse. "Colonel Nettles is unwell; this project is being shut down. Lower your weapons, this is just a protest. You all know me. *Lower your weapons.*"

Clay wanted to shout his relief as the soldiers glanced at each other and complied. The witch, satisfied, swung her sword back into its scabbard and rode back to the Treeman and the Captain. She looked at the cat and smiled.

"You have done well, I know of an old man who will be proud. Though he waits for you in Annwn, will you ride with me again?"

The Captain looked at the witch with sad yellow eyes. He felt that he might be looking at her for the last time.

"I will stay," he said, "to be sure that it is done well and then…"

"He will return," said the Treeman.

The witch nodded, leaned out of her saddle and kissed the cat on the head. She took the pouch and placed it around the Captain's neck.

"This was entrusted to me by the great Druid," she said, "he created the gateway for you. This is your key to Annwn, the Otherworld and to your immortality, to be passed to you on your final journey. The Followers will light your way to the gate. Good-bye and fare well bright star."

The Captain gave a little cry and the witch turned her horse. She started back down the hill and paused where Clay knelt next to Nettles who lay on his back, a dull and empty expression on his face.

Clay swallowed as she looked at him with dark eyes.

"Don't make me come back again."

"I will make good, I swear it," he said as he fixed her stare.

She nodded and walked on to where the soldiers knelt nursing their guns. The horse reared as she laughed.

"It's your lucky day, soldier boys," she called, and with that she spurred her horse down the hill and thundered back out onto the Roman road and into the distance.

Robert Clay became a tireless campaigner. Under the pressure of the public opinion that he garnered, the government relented and the missile site was scrapped at the Druid hill. The fences came down and the ditches were repaired. The concrete paths were removed and the buildings were taken away. He sold everything he had and raised money to purchase the site, this he placed in trust so that it would be protected and preserved for the future. The visitor's centre was converted into a centre for the hill and explored the rich mythology and history of the place. A space was set aside where he began a painstaking restoration of the Lightning Tree and the Captain watched in satisfaction when the day came for it to be returned to the hill top. He nestled in the Treeman's branches from a distance, as the huge crane delicately swung it back into place. A scaffold secured it as Clay spent a year, calling upon all his experience; working with a surgeon's skill to knit, secure and pin the damaged roots back together. At last the work was completed and the lighting tree once more crowned the sacred hill.

The warm sun was dipping low in the sky when he and the Captain walked to the summit on a summer's eve. Clay often wondered what would have happened to him had the Captain not paid him a visit at the inn that night. He loved the Captain.

They sat quietly together watching the sunset and the Captain turned to his friend.

"It is time for me to return," he said.

Clay felt his heart breaking, but he nodded, the Captain had told him that the time was coming.

"Don't be sad, Robert, I am returning to a beautiful place and to my oldest friend, my teacher.

Clay managed a smile and held the Captain in his arms, then he lifted him into the Lightning Tree, stroking the old cat's thick fur.

"I wish I knew that you were going to be…alright. If there was some way that I knew you were alright."

"You will know," said the Captain and with that he paused, looking at Clay with kind yellow eyes.

"One last thing, Robert, I thought you would like to know. The squirrel became a stag." Recognition flickered in Clay's mind and with that, the Captain blinked, flicked his tail and disappeared within the hidden hole where lightning had struck, so many, many years before.

Clay stood alone in the twilight. He felt an overwhelming loneliness and hot tears streamed down his cheeks. The Captain was gone. He sighed and slowly turned to leave, but something was different. He realized that the evening had become very still. The world around him seemed altered, silent and magical, outside of time. Behind him, he heard a whispering. Turning and looking up, he saw that the tree was forming a canopy of golden leaves. They shimmered and danced together against the darkening sky. They grew upon the branches and sent beams of golden light sparkling and revolving like stars around him and he wept again, this time, tears of pure joy. He watched, enraptured, as the leaves slowly faded and then he knelt and kissed the ground.

ABOUT THE AUTHOR

Simon Robinson is from Exeter, Devon in Britain. He is a historian, writer and entrepreneur who has developed and managed projects in the for-profit and non-profit worlds. Among other things he is the creator of "Pirates of Nassau" an interactive museum in the Bahamas as well as "FirstVoices" an online language tool used by native elders and youth around the world to archive endangered indigenous languages. He lives in Vancouver, Canada.